DOUBLE PLAY SUMMER

LATONYA RICHARDSON

LARICH MEDIA GROUP

DOUBLE PLAY SUMMER

LATONYA RICHARDSON

Dedicated to husband Anthony, and our children Jasmine, Anthony, Jr., Xavier, Ajia, Kye, and Torri, all multisport athletes. Through them, I experienced sports, great summers, and a lifetime of memories I will cherish forever.

Cover image by Traneisha Y. Jones &
designed by LaTonya Richardson

1

———

ight is her number
McKinley is her name
Yes, she is the reason
We're gonna win this game.

THE DUGOUT IS CHEERING and going crazy. The bases are loaded and Big Mac is up to bat. Although she's skinny, she got the nickname because she's a finisher. Known for being a clutch player, sending balls deep into center field. McKinley's hit the scoreboard at least five times this season and has knocked the ball over the fence at least six times. Someone from the stands once hollered Big Mac, and the name stuck.

It's a full count with two strikes, three balls at the bottom of the seventh inning, and we're down by two. If Big Mac lives up to her reputation, she'll bring us all home, and we'll win the game.

"Stay calm and focus," Coach Todd yelled from the coach's box.

The pitcher throws the ball, and *crack*! Big Mac sends the ball deep into center field right over the fence. Our dugout goes wild and they all run to home plate to welcome us in chanting:

Come home

Come home

We miss you

We miss you

Come home

Come home

"THAT'S THE BALL GAME!" The umpire yells.

It's shaping up to be the best summer ever! I'm playing my dream position and our team chemistry is the best it's ever been. Most of us have played together since twelve and under softball and we're genuine friends. Coach says you can't buy the kind of chemistry we've developed over the years.

I'll dream about this game for months to come. I

had four runs, made four outs, and almost a double play. Jade, my best friend and our first baseman, dropped the ball. But we're working on making that play work. By the big tournament, we should have mastered it. We're practicing, but game situations always come out different.

On the drive home, I gave a recap of the highlights to my family. They could barely get a word in. Mama finally said, "When we get home, we need to talk."

"ARE YOU KIDDING ME?" I said, dropping into a chair at the kitchen table. "But it's a big tournament for our team. Ma, it's a big tournament for me!"

"There will be more tournaments this summer and the next. There is more to life than playing softball. Gran's house is too much for her to take care of by herself, and her health has not been the best lately. She needs our help and we are going to give it to her. Our family is important and it comes first above everything else."

"What about Uncle Jaxon or Auntie Liv and their families? Can't they do it, or at least help? Why do we have to do it?"

"I can't count on either of them right now. Your dad and I have discussed it and our decision is final."

"And you never considered how your decision would impact me, or even how I'd feel about it? I've worked hard, really hard over, the last year to get better. And now that I've finally secured my position as shortstop, you're snatching the rug from under me. I'm not saying I don't want to help Gran, but can we do it after my tournament?"

"Don't be so dramatic, Daisy. We're all making sacrifices. And, I need you to move your things into your brother's room before we leave. When we return, I want the room to be ready for your Gran."

"D.J., Ma. Will you please call me D.J. all the time?"

From where I sit, it looks like I'm the only one making sacrifices around here. Gran is coming to live with all of us, but I'm having to give up my room and miss a crucial tournament. Other than my parents' bedroom, mine is the next largest, with an ensuite bathroom. Daddy says he wants Gran to have her privacy.

I have to move in with J.P., my nine-year-old brother. His room smells like old cheese, he farts in his sleep, and still has an imaginary friend. I'd be better off sleeping in a closet. Since I'm a girl, my older brother, J.R. and J.P. should share a room. My parents wouldn't even entertain the thought. So, I'm stuck.

Like I said before, I'm missing a crucial softball tournament. Mama thinks it's just another tournament in a summer of tournaments. It's so much more. I've worked my butt off to move from outfield to shortstop. I've practiced all year long, including during the off-season. I've always wanted to play shortstop since I first started playing when I was nine years old. Daddy took me to see a college softball game. Kattie Pierre was the shortstop. She was ridiculously good, catching balls and tagging runners between first and second base. Kattie stopped a ground ball, tagged second base, slung it to first, making a double play. From that day, I set my sights on playing shortstop just like her.

My coaches have always put me in the outfield because of my speed. Finally, Coach Todd gave me a chance to play in-field. So far this season, I've led our team in runs and outs. I haven't made a double-play yet, but I'm looking forward to that day. I don't want to let our team down.

This upcoming tournament is a game-changer for all of us. It's the *Super Summer Classic Showdown* in Chicago. The top two teams are guaranteed a bid to the Midwest Nationals in Chicago. Coach Todd says we have a good shot. Playing on that level is the kind of opportunity softball players only get in their dreams. And it can open doors that high school leagues can't. There will be college coaches from all over the U.S. looking for their next standout player. Although Kattie Pierre hasn't played for years, she still attends.

When we return to practice tomorrow, I will have to tell my teammates and coach, that I won't be going with them to the big tournament, and their shot at Nationals is basically in the hands of Mya.

"Bring it in ladies," Coach Todd yells to the team after the warm-up. "Listen up, D.J. has something she needs to share with us before practice."

"Share? I don't see any food. What's going on?" Jade joked, jogging over with the others trailing behind her.

"Yeah, what's up, shortstop?" someone else yelled.

Taking a deep breath, I squeezed my glove, trying to force myself to say the words. What I want to do is take the coward's way out and run home and text them the news. Daddy says you should deliver important and impactful news in person when possible; never by text. Here I am, in person, and still feeling like a coward.

"Cat got your tongue?" Jade asked. "Spill it, already."

"Okay, okay. I... uh. My Gran is coming to live with us; she can't live by herself anymore. Our family has to pack up her house and move her here. My mom says we all have to make sacrifices. The thing is, all of this is happening the same weekend as the big tournament... and I have to miss it."

"Are you kidding me?" Rosie, our pitcher, blurts. "D.J., do you know how hard we've all worked? And just like that, you back out."

Rosie's disappointment echoed through the crowd of girls.

"I know how hard we've all worked to get to where we are, and the *Super Summer Classic Showdown* is the best of the best. Listen, you all can do this without me. Just because I can't be there doesn't mean you have to give up. Right?"

"Yeah, right!" Mya stood clapping. "We've got this ladies. We're all more than capable of playing multiple positions. Let's go to Chicago and kick some butt. Who are we?"

"Diamond Dolls," the girls barely shouted.

"Who?" Mya yelled again.

"Diamond Dolls," they yelled louder.

"I can't hear yooooou!"

"THE DIAMOND DOLLS!" they responded thunderously.

"Alright ladies, we have work to do. Let's start with fielding drills. Stormy, you're on lead."

I just stood there as everyone scattered, not knowing what to do. And here comes Mya to rub it in.

"D.J., don't worry about a thing. I have shortstop covered for the tournament... and when you return. Take your time with your granny. We will miss you in Chicago."

"Wait a minute, D.J. Where do you think you're going? I'm not dismissing you from practice," coach stopped me.

"I thought you might not want me to practice since I won't be here for the tournament next weekend."

"You thought wrong. We still have a double-header this weekend. We're expecting you to play. I know you're bummed about not being able to take the trip with us, but you're needed in another role. I've preached time and time again that the team comes first. Your family is the team that needs you right now. Just as you are a key member of the Diamond Dolls, you have a greater role with your family. We'll miss you, but we'll be fine."

"Thanks, coach."

"Now, get out there."

"How did practice go?" Mama asked when I put my bike up after making it home.

"Ma, why are you lurking around out here?"

"Girl, I'm not lurking. I'm relaxing and enjoying the quiet with no one calling my name. Come here and join me. You didn't answer me. How did practice go?"

"It was practice," I said, joining mama on the patio. "I told the team I won't be joining them in Chicago for the big tournament."

"How did they take the news?"

"They were disappointed, but they'll be fine — I guess. Most of the team understood. Mya can't wait to play my position. She thinks she's going to keep it after the tournament. Newsflash, I'm loaning it to her, not giving it up. I've worked too hard to roll over and play dead."

"Your dad and I are sorry you have to miss this trip, but we need your help. With Gran coming to live with us, we will all have to make adjustments, especially Gran. Instead of looking at the situation as a loss, try to think positively. You'll get to spend more time with her, and I know she'll love it. When we'd visit her, the two of you seemed to have so much fun. With her being under the same roof, maybe you can do more of those things. I do want to warn you. Gran is starting to have difficulty remembering things now and then, and her health issues have made her a little fragile."

"I should go in. I've got a few things I need to do," I said getting up from the chair and heading to the back door. "Can I ask you a question?"

"Sure."

"What if I stayed with Jade's family, and—"

"D.J., I'm not entertaining anything else about Chicago. You're going with us, and this conversation is over. Do I make myself clear?"

"Yes, ma'am, crystal clear."

My three-step plan to convince Mama to change her mind about letting me go to Chicago just went out the window.

Step 1: Ask about staying with Jade and her family.
Step 2: Schmooze Daddy and let him convince her.

Step 3: Have Jade convince her mom to call and ask Mama.

Do I make myself clear? That means try me and you won't be playing anymore this summer. Yeah, mama didn't say those words, but I've learned to read between the lines. It looks like I'll be taking that trip to help Gran pack if I like it or not. I'm going, but I don't have to like it.

2
___

"Take those things off your ears, D.J., I've been calling your name for the past ten minutes." Mama fussed, as she stood in the doorway. "Do you need some help with your room?"

"Not right now," I sighed heavily, continuing to pack up my room in preparation for the next tenant, and trying to listen to Beyoncé in one ear. "Where will all of my things go in J.P.'s room? I have so much stuff."

"I made room for you, but it's not as much space as you have here in this room. I knew you would have a problem with deciding what you'll move. Let's try this. I saw it once on one of those organization reality shows. Make three piles; keep, throw away, and give away."

"Throw away? Are you serious? I don't plan to throw away anything."

"D.J., be reasonable. What about these cleats, they are beat up and old. You can start there."

"Absolutely not! Ma, these are my favorite cleats! I wore them when I hit my very first home run, successfully slid into second base for the first time, and tagged Lightening O'Guinn on her way to third base. That was an epic season, these cleats will always be special, and will never see the trash."

"Okay. Okay. I'm going to leave you to it. When you need my help, just yell. Good luck with this mess you've made," Mama said, backing out of the door.

I stood there looking into my closet, the drawers I pulled out, and the mound of clothes hiding my bed. Before I could finish thinking that I need a distraction, my phone rang—Jade to the rescue.

"Talk to me," I answered.

"You sound like you just lost your best friend. What's wrong?" Jade questioned.

"Everything to be exact, but right now, I'm staring at the mess in my bedroom, and I don't know what to pack up first."

"Pack up? You're moving down the hall to your little brother's room. Just move your stuff, not pack it up and unpack it. While you're at it, try throwing away some of that trash. I promise you are a hoarder in training. I've seen your room."

"You too? My mom just tried to get me to throw away my favorite cleats."

"Oh no! You mean the ones you wore when you hit your very first home run, and tagged Lightening O'Guinn out?"

"Yeah, and don't forget that I successfully slid into second base for the first time wearing those shoes," I reminded her.

"How could I ever forget that?"

"Exactly, and I hear the sarcasm in your voice. Cut it out."

"I'm glad you did. How many times have I heard the infamous story of those shoes? The point, is you need to get rid of some of the junk you call necessary. Your Gran will be here before you know it. I would come over and help, but I have this thing."

"A thing, Jade?"

"Umm, yeah. A family thing," she laughed. "Listen, I have to clean up my own room and I don't have the energy to argue with you about what to throw away in yours. At the end of each summer, before going back to school, my mom makes us declutter. We are allowed to keep several special things, like your cleats, and add them to our chest of memories. It's just a box, but we play along. We can only keep what can fit into the box. It's usually things we're still using and donate what we're not."

"I'll consider it," I said before ending the call. I pulled one drawer out of the dresser and proceeded to take it down the hall to J.P.'s room and dumped it on the twin bed I'll be occupying.

"It looks like you're just moving your mess from one place to the next," J.R. laughed, standing in the doorway of the bathroom. "From the looks of it, you'll be moving that mound of crap when Gran moves in. By the way, I caught a little of your practice the other day. You're hesitating before you throw the ball to first base. Don't think about it. Just throw."

"Really? Are you giving advice? How many games has your team won this season? You all are like the *Bad News Bears*. When your team starts winning, then come back and give me a lesson or two."

"Don't get a bigger head," shooting a rubber band directly towards my face.

"Maaa, make J.R. go away!" I yelled.

"No need for tattling. I'll leave you to your work."

J.R. is an excellent baseball player, football player, soccer player, and probably any other sport he'd try. He's what my dad calls a natural athlete. Me, on the other hand, I'm just good at softball.

Finally, I was left alone with my music and chaos to condense my whole life from my large bedroom to what amounts to the space of a walk-in closet. I carried my belongings down the hall one laundry basket load and a couple of songs at a time. After five times of the back and forth shuffle down the hall, I started to think twice about trashing a few things, starting with the box of erasers I found buried in the back of the closet.

In third grade, I was obsessed with gum erasers, and Guinness World Records. I wanted to set a world record for the largest collection of gum erasers. If I found one, I'd add it to my collection. At that time, I was finding at least one a week, sometimes more. When kids in my class dropped them on the floor, I'd swoop in and snatch them right up. For some reason, I thought I had hundreds of erasers. There are about twenty in this box, and none of them are new.

I still dream about setting or breaking a world record. It just won't be for the largest collection of gum erasers.

Though I've moved almost all of the things into J.P.'s room, filled several garbage bags with junk, and created a pretty large pile of gently used items to take to the women's shelter, this room is still very much a mess. Mama wants to paint the room for Gran so I have to finish moving that it can be done.

J.P. was at a friend's house. I don't know if it's luck, or Mama had the wisdom of making sure he was out of the way. Still, he made sure I knew he wasn't happy with the arrangement, either. He used painters tape and divided the bedroom into his side and my side. That division is not equal. He clearly and intentionally left me with less space. Honestly, I can't even be mad; I would probably do the same.

I've moved my last load and I am exhausted. Now the problem is, which room will I sleep in tonight? Both beds are piled high with clothes and dare I say junk. There are several options; move the clothes over on the bed in my old room, sleep in the bathtub, or on the air mattress that seeps. The last time I slept on that air mattress, I woke up during the night because my back was hurting. I was on the floor.

It looks like I'll be sleeping next to a mound of clothes.

3

We left at six this morning. Mornings are not my thing, at all. I made myself comfortable on the back row of mama's SUV, put my headphones on, and pretended to be asleep. Though I didn't always have my music on, I kept the headphones on to keep my family from talking to me. It's my silent protest for having to make this trip, instead of going to Chicago with the team.

I was holding out hope that mama and daddy would change their minds before the team bus left. I had even dreamt about it. Mama came into my room to ask about my bags and to hurry before the team left without me. Clearly, my dream was a nightmare. Here I am in the back of the vehicle trying to act like I'm some-where else.

My game day playlist is all I want to listen to right now.

When Jade texted me to let me know they were leaving, my heart sank. There are no words for how empty and left out I feel.

Jade: It sucks that you're not with us. We're going to miss you, and I really wish your parents would have changed their minds. Mya says she's ready to fill in for you, but I'm not sure she's even convinced of it herself.

Me: Yep, it sucks big time. I miss you guys too, and Mya will be fine. The team has to show confidence in her, and she'll have it in herself. Gas her up a little and she'll perform when it's time.

Jade: Thanks, D.J. I'll keep you posted on our games.

Me: You're welcome, and please do!

Instead of playing the most important softball tournament of my life this weekend, I'll be packing up a house and moving my Gran.

WHEN WE ARRIVE at Gran's house, like most time, she's sitting on the porch waiting for us. Grand-daddy used to be the one waiting. After he died, when I was ten, Gran took over. "Your granddaddy said he wanted you guys to know you are welcome and that we've missed you," Gran said was the reason why they waited on the porch.

Just as expected, when we turned onto the road leading to her house, I could see her in the distance. As much frustration as I feel about having to be here, my heart smiled when I spotted her. Only my heart because I refused to show any outward indication I was excited about anything that has to do with this trip.

Gran greets each of us with her big smile and even bigger hug. Not the church hug, with the lean in and pat-pat. She wraps her arms around us and squeezes, just the right amount of tight.

"Hello Daisy. It's so good to see you, my sweet girl. Take those headphones off so I can see what you look like," Gran said, smiling. "I'm sorry you're missing the big tournament on account of me. I love you for making the sacrifice."

"You're welcome?" I said questioningly. "And Gran, everyone calls me D.J."

"Everyone but me. You will always be my Daisy. D.J. sounds like a boy's name, and you've always been my little flower."

I make my way to a seat on the porch while everyone else goes in the house. I'm not quite ready to go inside. Gran's house is always too hot, winter, spring, summer and fall. It doesn't matter what season. During the summer, she only turns on the air at night, when she has company. She says she's fine with the windows open and the ceiling fan. At Thanksgiving last year, daddy said it was so hot in the house, he was starting to melt like candles on a birthday cake. He spends most of his time on the porch cooling off.

Jade: Hey D.J., we made it to Chicago, and this hotel is amazing! After opening ceremony tonight, coach is taking us to dinner at Giordano's for pizza.

Me: That's cool. Eat a slice for me, and take plenty of pictures.

Jade: Wish us luck for tomorrow's game, we play at ten in the morning. We're already a bundle of nerves.

Me: Of course, I wish you guys the best. You all got this. Encourage everyone to rest well so that they will be fresh tomorrow, and stay away from the pool.

Go Diamond Dolls!

"Let's get to it," I yell, walking into the house.

We're on a mission. I'm ready to get this house packed up.

"I just drove for five hours and I'm tired." Daddy said with his face in his phone. "All I want to do is eat something and relax awhile."

"A few of the women from church have helped me pack a few things and we started with the kitchen," Gran said. "There's not a thing to eat. Someone is coming in the morning to pick up the fridge."

Surveying the house, I see that the kitchen and the den have boxes and the rest of the house is untouched. "Meeting in the living room," J.R. said, sneaking up on me. "Mama said it's time to go over the plan."

Mama is a planner. She plans everything; her days, our trips, and meals. Even her plans have plans. She has several planners; one for her job, one for our family activities, and another one for her organizations. How she keeps up with all of that is a mystery. One thing for certain, and two things for sure, mama has a plan for the packing of Gran's house. Things will get done in what she calls an orderly and efficient manner.

"We're starting this mission this evening— every child pairs with an adult. J.R., you're with me. J.P., you're with your dad. D.J., you're with Gran," mama assigned.

"Yay," Gran cheered and winked at me.

"But Gran, I wanted to be with you," J.P. whined.

"I need you, son," Daddy said. "I'm looking forward to us working together, starting with securing dinner for the family."

"Okay, here's the plan. In the room you're working in, make a give-away pile and a throw away pile. The keep pile will then be divided into take with us and move to storage. Alright, we're going to work until dinner and then about two hours after dinner. Tomorrow, we'll start again."

Gran and I went to our designated room, the room in the back of the house that has been used more for storage than a bedroom.

"Gran," I said when we walked in. "It's going to take us untill the middle of next week to pack up this room."

"Come on now, Daisy. It's not as bad as it looks," Gran responds.

"Gran," I groaned. She refuses to call me D.J. I don't know what she sees in this room, but it's going to be a lot of work.

"Trash, trash, trash, trash, keep. Trash, keep, keep, trash," Gran said, getting started.

It looks like most of the things in this room is going to be trashed. Packing up this room might not be so bad after all. It's a lot of old junk. We can get this room done and move on. I started singing, "Trash, trash, trash," with everything I touched.

"Whoa," Gran yelled! "What are you doing? That's not trash."

"But it's an old dusty clock, older than some of the things you said are trash. I doubt this thing even works."

"No, it doesn't work. You're right, it's older than anything else in this room other than that rocking chair in the corner, and that's not trash either."

"I don't get it, Gran. It's super old, doesn't work, dusty, and it's not trash?"

"Exactly," she said, taking a seat. "After I was born, my mama was ill and had to take medicine. My papa had to work and couldn't be there to give it to her. He bought her this clock, and it chimed every hour on the hour. She'd wake up to see if it was time for her to take more medicine. You see, this clock was bought the day after I was born. It's just as old as I am, and is what you would call an heirloom. Papa paid a week's wages to buy this clock. Like this clock, I'm old, don't work as well as I used to, and even a bit dusty, but I'm not ready to be thrown out with the trash yet."

"Okay, Gran, I get it. I'll put it in the keep and take with us pile, if that's okay?" I reason.

"Good idea."

We worked together separating items into piles. Still, the trash pile grew larger than the others.

"Dinner's here," daddy called. I'm so happy to hear those words. It's not *Giordano's* in Chicago, but it's tonight's dinner.

4

———

It's day two of packing and I'm up early, before everyone else enjoying quiet time on the porch. To be honest, I didn't sleep much last night. I was tossing and turning, watching the clock for what seemed like every hour on the hour. My mind is in Chicago with my team. My only thought is that they are about to play today without me. Right now, I imagine them suiting up in their uniforms, putting on their game faces, and listening to their hype music.

SINCE TWELVE AND UNDER SOFTBALL, I've made a playlist to listen to before games. No matter how my playlist changes from year-to-year, Nelly's *Heart of a*

Champion will always be first in the rotation. My brother is responsible. Every morning of one of his games, especially football, he'd fill the whole house with that song. We'd all be singing while getting ready for our day. When I started making my own game day playlist, that song was an obvious and necessary choice.

ALTHOUGH I MAY NOT BE PLAYING with my team today, I will still listen to my playlist, while I know they're getting ready, and shoot them a good luck text.

ME: *Good morning, team. While you all are getting ready to play this morning, I want*

you to know I'm with you in spirit. We've all practiced very hard for this moment, and it's time to execute. Go out there today and leave it all on the field, win, lose, or draw.

WIN DIAMOND DOLLS!

JADE: *Thanks, D.J., for the encouraging words.*

. . .

STORMY: We wish you could be here; I'll miss you on my right side.

MYA: I got shortstop covered D.J. and promise not to let you down.

TURNING my music up in my ears, I danced to my hype music. No one's watching, and it feels good to let loose and release all of my pent-up energy.

"What on earth are you doing?" Gran asked, laughing.

"How long have you been standing there?" I yanked my earphones off and sat down.

"Long enough," she said handing me a cup of hot cocoa. "Mind if I sit with you and enjoy the morning?"

We sat and sipped in quiet. Gran knows how much I love her hot chocolate. Not the hot chocolate that you buy in the box. She uses powdered cocoa, milk, cream and sugar to make the best hot chocolate I've ever tasted. No matter what time of the year, Gran's hot chocolate always hits the spot. Several times, she's walked me through making it step-by-step. But when I'm not with her, it doesn't come out the same. Gran's hot chocolate fixes everything, or at least it used to.

"Tell me something," Gran finally breaks the silence. "Are you worried about your team?"

"I don't know if I'm more worried or concerned. We have a great chemistry, feeding off each other's strengths and weaknesses. Coach says we've become a well-oiled machine. The thing is, when one part of that machine is down or not functioning properly, it affects the rest. We've come to depend on each other to fulfill our part to keep the machine running. Do I think they can win without me? Yes, I do. But do they know they can win without me, is the bigger question. The last time we had a big game and one of us was not there, we fell apart."

"We've got a lot to do today, are you ready?" Gran started for the door.

"Yes, ma'am, but can I ask you something first?"

"Sure, sugar."

"How do you feel about leaving your home?"

"You're the first person to ask me that. I was starting to think no one cared how I felt at all. Don't get me wrong; your mama and daddy, as well as your aunt and uncle, have my best interest in mind.

Living by myself isn't the best thing for me anymore, but no one asked me. They told me what would happen, and I just went along to get along. I've never lived any other place, and I'll be leaving behind a lot of memories, loved ones, and friends, and I'm sad about that."

"I'm sorry, Gran, that you're sad. Is there anything I can do to help you make this transition better for you?"

"Actually, yes. Yes, there is. Let's go for a walk."

"Right now?" I asked. "But you just said we have a lot to do."

Gran gave me the eye and I moved toward the steps where she was standing. We started walking down the road that used to look like it stretches for miles, and Gran grabbed my hand. We walked like old friends.

Gran's house sits at the top of a hill at the end of the road, and it's surrounded by woods, a large open field, and more woods. She led me to a path behind the house, and we walked for what felt like a mile and stopped.

"Right here is where my mama and daddy's house used to sit; a four-room house. In that house, my parents raised five children. We didn't have much, but we had a lot of love. And over there, we had a chicken coop. It was my responsibility to collect eggs. I was terrified of snakes. If anything moved, I'd jump and run. Many days, I left eggs behind. My older brother would go behind me and get the eggs so I wouldn't get in trouble."

We laughed and walked some more. I didn't say a word, just listened to Gran reminisce. She went on and on, and I took it all in, just like a good girlfriend.

"Before your granddaddy left for the armed service, we had a picnic right under this tree," she laughed. "He tried to carve our initials in it, but his knife was so dull. It slipped and nicked the back of his hand. Lord, he bled so much. I thought he was gonna pass out. He laid here on the ground untill he stopped feeling sick and made me swear never to tell a soul. You're the first person I've ever told.

The path stops here now and it has grown up over the years. Further back, there was a stream my brothers and sisters and I used to play in. Those were fun times. They all moved away to chase their dreams. This way of life became too slow. But I stayed, hanging on. Everything on this hill, forty acres, belongs to me, which means it belongs to you."

"What do you want me to do with it, Gran?"

"Anything you want, Daisy, but promise me never to sell it. Chester Hill has been in our family since our ancestors were freed from slavery. It's named for Chester Brantley, my grand daddy's granddaddy. Promise me, Daisy."

"I promise, Gran," I reassured her.

"We'd better get back to the house before your mama sends out a search party for us. Did you bring your brand-new driver's license with you?"

"Yes, ma'am, I sure did."

"Good girl," she said, grabbing my hand again. "Later, I'll need you to take me somewhere to say goodbye to a few people. I don't know when the next time I'll be back here."

"Of course, Gran," I said, squeezing her hand.

At that moment, I felt closer to Gran than I ever remembered. Right now, we share a secret and a pact. We walk back slowly, enjoying each other's company and the cool of the morning.

"Where have you two been? Mama's looked all over for you and called your phone, D.J. She was threatening to call the police," J.P. greeted us on the porch.

"We just went for a walk, that's all. Tell your

mama to calm down and take a chill pill. Ain't that what you kids say?"

"No, ma'am. No one says that, and you won't ever say it again," We laughed.

The two of us went back to our designated room and picked up where we left off yesterday. We sorted the contents into throwaway, giveaway, keep for storage, or to take piles. So far, our biggest pile is still the throwaway pile.

Hours passed and it looked like we were making progress until Gran started adding more and more to the keep pile. Most of the things had more sentimental value than anything else. But I was not going to be the one to tell her she couldn't keep it. After our walk this morning, I realized this move is going to be difficult for her. And if more than a few sentimental pieces from her life is what she wants, she should have them. But of course, my mama has the last say.

"What about this box?" I held it in the air for her to see.

"That's a keeper to take for sure! I've looked for that box several years ago and had no idea where it was. My memory has failed me so and I didn't think I'd ever see it again. In fact, I thought it had already been thrown away. Please hand it to me," Gran said, walking towards me.

"What's so special about that box?" I asked.

"Baby, the box ain't special; it's the contents of this box that mean so much to me. I told you your granddaddy was in the armed services, the Marines to be exact. While he was away training and then in the Vietnam War, we wrote to each other." She opened the box to show me the contents. "I told you he didn't have nothing, not a thing, but he was great with words. He wrote me letters whenever he could, and in return, I'd write him back. I sent him a letter every week. Whenever he was able to get mail, he always had several letters waiting for him. Then I didn't hear from him for two months. I was frantic and thought he was dead. Finally, a letter came. He was in the hospital and hurt pretty bad. You don't want to hear about all of that. In this box are the letters he sent me, along with his Purple Heart, other medals, and pictures of him in his uniform."

"Wow, a Purple Heart," I held it in my hand. "I've heard of this medal, but never seen one in real life."

"Yep, your granddaddy was something else. It's time we make that trip that I told you about this morning. Grab your license and meet me in my car."

"Right away."

"And Daisy. Don't tell your mama we're leaving, you hear?"

"Yes, ma'am," I did as she said.

I was excited. This was fun, like old times when Gran and I would sneak off. We'd usually end up at the grocery store for whatever she needed for dinner or dessert. Of course, I'd always get a treat. But I still had to bring back something for my brothers and cousins.

Having Gran around all the time is going to be fun. Mama warned that she might be a little different. I haven't seen any difference, not that I can tell anyway.

5

"Just announce that we're leaving, why don't you?" Gran laughed. "You slammed the door so loud, it could have been an alarm."

"I'm sorry," I cringed, looking for someone to come out of the house and catch us. The door did slam pretty loudly.

"Now drive slow, and when we get past those trees, step on it."

"Aye aye, captain." I did just as Gran instructed.

"Girl, you drive like a bat out of hell," Gran laughed. "You should be a NASCAR driver instead of playing softball."

"You drive pretty fast yourself," I laughed.

Gran navigated to our destination, telling me when to turn, while pointing out different things and waving at people she knew and a few she didn't.

"Where are we going again?" I ask.

"I told you earlier, there are a few people I want to say goodbye to," she said, looking out the window.

"Pull over," Gran yelled abruptly, causing me to swerve. "Stop and get out with me!"

"Get out? Get out for what?"

"Use your complicated phone, camera, or a computer and take my picture right here," Gran insisted. "I want to have a memory of this place always, even when I can't remember."

"Pose," I tell her, and she just puts a hand on her hip and smile. "Come on. Give me a little sass. Alright, hip action. Now pucker your lips and give me a peace sign."

"Enough," she laughed. "I'm out here looking like a crazy person, but the impromptu photoshoot was fun. This diner, *Four Forks*, was the very first place I worked, and it holds great memories."

"*Four Forks*? That's a crazy name for a diner. Was it a greasy spoon or did it have good food?"

"Yes, the name was a little different, but it had *the* best food! People drove miles to eat at *Four Forks*. Lunch, dinner and dessert; it was all good, all the time. Everything was homemade, nothing boxed, frozen, or premade. My favorite was the fried pies. No matter how much I've tried, I still can't get my crust to be as light and crunchy as theirs."

"Your fried pies are the best, Gran. When we get back to our house, will you please make them?"

"Of course, I'd love to. It's been a while since I've made any, don't know how the pies will turn out. We should get going. It's been great reminiscing. They're waiting for me."

We drove for another couple of minutes, with Gran telling more stories about the *Four Forks Diner*. Part of me is convinced she made that name up, but I'll give it to her. I was starting to recognize the route we're taking.

"Gran, why are we pulling up to the church? They didn't wait for you," I announced the obvious.

"No. We're right on time," she said, sounding very sure of herself.

"But, ain't nobody here to say goodbye to."

"Park over there by the big tree, near the gate."

"And for what? The only thing over there is the graveyard."

"Exactly," she said, opening the door. "The people I need to say goodbye to are in the graveyard. Come on. Get out."

"I'll sit right here," I said, looking around. "With the car running."

"Daisy, get out of the car and join me. There are a few people I want you to meet," she said with the authority of telling and not asking. "And turn the car off."

"Yes, ma'am," I responded hesitantly. I've heard mama and daddy low talking about Gran's condition, and now I'm wondering if she has lost her mind. But I went with her anyway. I guess I've lost my mind too.

"GRAN, they say you're not supposed to walk on someone's grave. It may bring you bad luck or something," I said nervously while walking behind her trying my best not to step on anyone's grave.

"Is that right," she said and kept right on marching. "I want to start further in the back and make my way back to the car. I guess there are a few things you should know. I'm almost sure your mama hasn't told you."

"That church and the property this graveyard sits on was all started by one of our ancestors, Bernard Caillouet. After he was freed from slavery, he and his family built a church and school here on the property that his former master gave to him. This church and graveyard have been in operation since to take in *our* people. It's one of only a few surviving black cemeteries in this part of the state. We're almost there."

"Gran, I read that slaves couldn't read, and it was against the law to teach them to read. So why would he start a school if no one could read to teach the others?" I had a headful of questions then.

"Bernard Caillouet was responsible for taking his master's children to school every day. While sitting in the back of the schoolhouse waiting for them all day, he learned a thing or two. Eventually, he became the teacher of this school. He and his family are out here in this graveyard somewhere. Probably way down that hill. There are no grave markings to know exactly, and trees have grown up. We've made it to my family's burial plot. Here's my mama and daddy, meet your great grandparents, Daisy and Edward Caillouet. Mother and Papa, meet my Daisy."

"Wow," was all I could say.

"Yes, all the Daisies in our family have been women to reckon with," Gran said proudly. "My mother was a midwife. She said she birthed a ton of babies. One time, when I was little, I remember one of the neighbors sent for her to help her cow birth a calf. She used to tell that story often. Do you still tell that story in Heaven, Mother?"

Gran knelt down in front of her parents' graves and laid her head over on their *stones* she called them. With her eyes closed, she started speaking just above a whisper. I couldn't understand. But she seemed to be in deep conversation with saying her goodbyes. When she finished, she kissed the stone, got up, and walked a few feet.

"Over here is one of my favorite cousins, Caroline. We were like bread and butter my papa used to say. She was my cousin and my best friend. We were inseparable until she married, and they moved away. I was sick without her. She would come back every summer and always had something for me from Detroit. Then she just quit coming. Several years later, we found out she had been sick. Her brother went there and got her and brought her back home to me. I helped her mama nurse her until she died. And we buried her right out here. Somebody said she died of a broken heart. The reason she stopped coming home every summer to visit is her husband left her and ran off with another woman. She didn't want us to know, and she grieved over losing him untill she grieved herself to death."

Gran stood up, shook her head, and patted the little stone that marked her cousin's grave. "Goodbye, sweetie," she whispered.

I continued to follow in her footsteps as she touched headstones and whispered to herself and introducing me to a few more along the way. Finally, we reached Oscar 'Oc' Bergeron, and she took the scarf from her shoulders, placed it on the ground, and sat on it.

"Hey Oc. It's a beautiful day. I'm here with Daisy. She's grown up so much and looking just like her mama. Say hey to your papa, Daisy. And if you would give me a few minutes alone with him. Go on back to the car. I'll be there shortly."

I walked back to the car slowly, every few steps turning around to check on Gran. I've always thought of her as strong, like a superwoman, but today, she seemed so fragile. It was as if I was seeing her for the first time in a very long time. Vulnerable and sad. No one else has even noticed her smile is a little crooked.

Right here and right now, I'm appointing myself as Gran's keeper, making this transition easy for her. She would do the same for me.

Watching and waiting for Gran to come out of the graveyard, my mind goes to Chicago and my team. Grabbing my phone, I scroll through the pictures my teammates sent of last night's opening ceremony. Jealousy is not my thing, but I am feeling some kind of way about not being there. A little salty perhaps, but definitely not jealousy.

The game should have been over long before now and I'm antsy to know if they won or not. What I really want to know is if Mya was able to hold my position down. Daddy tells me often if you want to know something, ask.

I start a text message to Jade and delete it. Five times. That's how many versions of the text I wrote before finally sending. The final test was one letter.

Me: W?

As soon and I pressed send, I threw my phone in the seat and got out of the car, making my way to Gran. I was too nervous to know if it was a W or an L. I felt sick just thinking about it.

"Slow down," Gran grabbed me by the shoulders when I made it to her. "You're running, breathing hard, and eyes bucked like you saw a ghost. Although we're in a cemetery, everyone here is dead and can't hurt you."

"I just wanted to make sure you're okay," I managed to say.

"I'm fine," she shrugged. "Gonna miss them all terribly."

Although her family and friends have been gone for quite a while, I understood exactly what she meant. As we leave the cemetery, I make small talk about nothing in particular, trying to make Gran smile and take her mind off the move and leaving her whole life behind.

"AND WHERE DID you two runaways sneak off to this time?" Mama questioned, as we walked in the door.

"Just saying goodbye to family and friends," I answered winking at Gran to let her know I had her back.

Just like that, the two of us go back to packing, laughing, and talking about the memories we'll make together once we get back home. To be honest, I'm looking forward to it, starting with those fried pies she promised.

"Who is this lady in this picture?" I asked. It looked like it could be Gran, but I wasn't sure. The picture was black and white, and the young lady looked like a movie star.

"That's me," she smiled proudly, posing like the picture. "It was my twenty-first birthday. I saved six months for that dress, hat, and shoes. When I saw it in a catalog, and I knew I wanted the whole outfit. The model had that same pose."

"So, where did you go dressed so fancy?"

"Child, nowhere but to the *Four Forks Diner*," Gran laughed. "But I was the most well-dressed customer that evening. I kept that outfit long past it's wear, until finally, I used it in a quilt. Come to think of it, I haven't seen that quilt in a long time. I want to take it, and a few other ones that are special to me."

While she left the room in search of her quilts, I reached for my phone. I heard the notifications on our way back from the cemetery, but I couldn't bring myself to look. Just as I expected, it was a text from Jade and Big Mac.

Jade: L! We play again in the losers bracket this evening at 4 p.m.

Big Mac: Our first round of play was TERRIBLE! We lost by five runs to a team we should have beat with no problems. We missed big plays, batted awfully, and our chemistry was completely off. There is no one person to blame. We all sucked.

And just so you know, Mya is struggling in your position, her confidence is shot. Keep us in your thoughts for this evening's game.

"I found several of the quilts I want to take," Gran announced, entering the room again. "What's going on? What changed since I left the room?"

"My team lost today and they're going to the loser's bracket. Mya is playing my position as shortstop and struggling. I feel responsible because I can't be there. We have a real shot at the national tournament, Gran. Like I told you, our team is a well-oiled machine and one of the parts is missing. I'm that part. Last year, we lost when another member of our team couldn't be there, and that tournament was not as important. They can win without me, they just have to have the confidence to do so."

"I'm so sorry to hear about your team's loss, Daisy. So, what are you going to do about it?"

"What do you mean? I'm here with you, hours away from Chicago, and helping to pack up your house. There is nothing I can do."

"There is always something you can do, Daisy. Think, what else can you do to get your team out of the rut they're in?"

"Honestly, I don't have a... You're right, Gran. There is something I can do. I'll be back in a few minutes."

I grabbed my phone and headed to the porch, dialing Mrs. Collins, Jade's mom. She's always the mom in the dugout helping keep stats. The phone rings several times.

"Shoot, voice mail," I sighed out loud.

"Yes, ma'am. How're they doing?" I said when I answered Mrs. Collins' call as soon as she called back.

"Hey, D.J. We're in the bottom of the second, and they're starting to fall apart already. They've given up five runs by making simple mistakes. We have two outs. It was two up, two down, and Big Mac is up to bat," Mrs. Collins fills me in.

"It's awfully quiet in the dugout. *Hit It. Rip It. Knock it Out!*" I yelled into the phone.

I hear my teammates repeat and finish the chant.

Hit It. Rip It. Knock It Out!

Hit It. Rip It. Knock It Out!

Knock that pitcher off the mound!

Knock that pitcher off the mound!

AND THEN IT HAPPENED, a clack of the bat hitting the ball.

"It's going. It's going to the fence!" Mrs. Collins yelled.

I jump to my feet, screaming to the top of my lungs on the porch. Everyone in the dugout is cheering.

D.J. we miss you

Come home

Come home

D.J. we miss you

We miss you

Come home

Come home

· · ·

THAT CHEER MEANS ONE THING; Big Mac hit a home run and I can now breathe.

"WHAT IN THE world is going on out here," Mama, daddy, and my brothers rushed to the porch.

"BIG MAC JUST HIT A HOME RUN!" I screamed some more.

"D.J., I've gotta go. We'll let you know how things turn out. Thanks, babe for calling. You always know exactly how to motivate the girls and get them going."

"THANKS, Mrs. Collins. I look forward to hearing about the win."

"SEE, I TOLD YOU," Gran said when I walked back into the room to continue to help her pack. "There is always something you can do."

. . .

"YOU DID TELL ME," I smiled. "Thank you."

BEFORE WE KNEW IT, we were done packing the house. Everything that's going with Gran back to our house will be loaded in a *U-Haul*. Tomorrow, daddy and the boys are taking the things Gran wants to keep in storage. Uncle Pete, who isn't an uncle at all, and his sons are coming to haul off the trash, take the donation pile to *Goodwill* and a women's shelter.

"CAN you believe we're ahead of schedule?" Mama said, looking around. "I am so proud of all of you and the way we've worked on packing up this house. D.J., I owe you a special thank you. I know you wanted to be somewhere else. It is a big sacrifice."

OUT OF NOWHERE, my phone started to explode with text notifications. I took a deep breath and held it, afraid of what all the commotion could be about.

MRS. COLLINS:WE won!

·   ·   ·

JADE:*IT's a win!*

STORMY: *Thanks, shortstop, you pulled us out of our rut! We owe you big time.*

ZOE: *We won!*

COACH TODD: *Thanks, D.J. Even miles away, you're still holding this team together. We miss you, kiddo.*

BIG MAC: *Thanks, I needed that. The team needed that. Mya held her own this game. Right up till she fractured her hand. Yep, she fractured her hand, and it was the coolest thing ever!*

SHE GOT CAUGHT *in a game of chicken, between second and third base. Running back to second, she slid on her belly with her left hand leading the way, jamming straight into the bag. With all the excitement, she didn't know anything was wrong until she made it home. We have another game in the losers bracket to work our way back to the winner's bracket. London is coming off the bench to play shortstop.*

"I'M SORRY THEY LOST AGAIN," Gran said, rubbing my back. "I was rooting for a win."

"THEY DIDN'T LOSE," I said.

"YOU DON'T LOOK like someone whose team just won," J.R. said.

"MYA FRACTURED her hand and London is coming off the bench to play shortstop. They have to win the next game on Sunday morning to make it back to the winner's circle," I explained.

FEELING DEFEATED ALL OVER AGAIN, I dug my glove out of my backpack and sat on the porch with my headphones on, playing the saddest song I could find, Boyz 2 Men's *End of the Road*. My pity-party was in full effect.

7

Yesterday, Gran said there is always something that can be done. I did the only thing left for me to do, send London a text with encouraging words and basic pointers.

ME: Hey London, stepping up to play shortstop on such short notice might be a little

nerve-wrecking, but I want you to know you can do it. You've played several different positions because you adapt to change very well, and Sunday morning will be no different. If you keep these three tips in mind, you'll do just fine.

.   .   .

TIP 1: Cover third base when the third baseman is fielding the ball. Be ready to receive the ball and tag the runner from second base out.

TIP 2: Cover second base when the second baseman is fielding the ball. Be ready to receive the ball and tag the runner from first base.

TIP 3: If you're fielding a ground ball, don't hesitate. The play is at first base.

GOOD LUCK ON SUNDAY.

LONDON: Thanks, D.J., your confidence in me means so much. I'm going to give it my best.

"I'VE LOOKED ALL over the house for you. I should have known I'd find you on the porch," daddy laughed, joining me. "There has been a change of plans. Uncle Pete is going to take care of the storage and the donations. We're going to load what we can in the *U-Haul* and head out shortly after noon."

"WHY THE CHANGE?" I asked.

"SINCE WE FINISHED AHEAD of schedule, Gran asked that we leave earlier."

"CAN I ASK YOU A QUESTION?"

"SURE, D.J. WHAT'S UP?"

"I KNOW mama said Gran hadn't been herself lately, and to me, she seems fine mostly. But do you think she seems a little sad?"

"TO BE HONEST, I haven't noticed with all the packing going on. It wouldn't be unusual for someone to be a little sad about leaving behind the only home they've ever known. In my non-professional opinion, it's expected. Wouldn't you think?"

"IT DOES MAKE SENSE. I just want to make sure Gran is okay and this move causes the least amount of stress on her."

"I'M sure Gran and your mother will appreciate your thoughtfulness. You're really sweet, Daisy," dad laughed.

"DAD. IT'S D.J."

"YES, MA'AM."

"DID you know that Gran's mom was named Daisy? And there were other Daisies in her family. All of them have made great contributions."

. . .

"YES, of course, I knew. That's exactly why you are named Daisy. Your mother is proud of her family history, and I'm looking forward to what you will add to that legacy. Here comes Uncle Pete. Let me warn your Gran."

"UNCLE PETE," I smiled, waiting for him to tickle me. The two of us have been playing that same game since I was a very little girl. I'd speak, and soon as he got close enough to me, he'd tickle my neck.

"HEY THERE, Jonathan and Daisy. Heard you all are taking your Gran away from us," he smirked as he stepped onto the porch, reaching to shake daddy's hand.

"YES, it's time we looked after her," Daddy said.

"MISS DAISY, make sure you take real good care of your Gran. This hill won't be the same without her and she will be missed," Uncle Pete said.

. . .

"PETE, I thought you'd never get here," Gran came out smiling. "Come on in; I have a few instructions about all of this stuff in here."

"YES, BOSS, I'M COMING," he laughed and followed Gran.

IT DIDN'T TAKE her long to give Uncle Pete his orders. He then helped daddy and the boys load the *U-Haul*. Several of Gran's friends, church members, and her pastor came by this morning to say their goodbyes. She hugged them all. Several of them brought her cards and food for our trip.

GRAN LOCKED up and walked the path behind the house, saying one last goodbye to her home, and all of its memories. We've made this trip before with Gran, but this time, she's coming to stay.

. . .

"ARE YOU READY?" I whispered to her as she stood in the front yard with her hands on her hips.

"READY OR NOT, HERE WE GO," she whispered back.

THIS TIME, I didn't sit in the far back; instead, I sat next to Gran, and I put my head on her shoulder. She closed her eyes like she didn't want to see the house disappear in the distance. I could feel her heart beating fast and hard, and her breathing heavy. Mama kept looking back at her with a worried face. She wanted to say something to Gran, but she read my eyes,which were asking her not to say anything. Finally, mama leaned over, stretching her arm to the back seat, and patted Gran's knee. Gran put her arm around me and held me tightly. The quiet of the ride, the hum of the vehicle, and the comfort of Gran put me to sleep like a milk wasted baby. We rode like that for what seemed like hours.

8

"Wake up, we're here," mama announced.

"Here? Where is here?" J.P. asked, yawning, stretching, and scratching. It never fails, no matter the time of day he wakes up, J.P. is going to yawn, stretch, and scratch. What he scratches is always a surprise. Some scratches are funnier than others.

"We've stopped for the night," Gran reassured.

"For the night? But why aren't we home?" He asked more questions.

"We have business to take care of tomorrow," Daddy said in a tone that said, don't ask again.

Never have we ever stopped at a hotel traveling to Gran's house or going back home. This stop has me a little suspicious of what's going on. Right now, I don't care. After sleeping on the sofa bed at Gran's with the springs poking me everywhere and then leaning on Gran's arm has my body very stiff and I have a crick in my neck. Any bed will work right now. Grabbing my backpack, I followed my family inside the hotel.

"D.J., let me talk to you for a minute," Daddy directs me to the sofa in the lobby while everyone else heads to the elevator.

"What's up, Daddy? This is a nice hotel."

"Yes, it is," he laughed.

"Do you have any idea where we are?"

"Not at all," I said, trying to figure out what he's getting at. "Daddy, I'm exhausted. All that packing took a little something out of me. Can we finish this upstairs?"

"Do you think you have enough left for a softball game?" He asked.

"Softball? What are you talking about?"

"No way," I whispered, looking around and spotting a banner *Welcome Midwest Region Super Summer Classic Showdown.* " Are we here to watch the next game?"

"Not exactly, D.J. We're here so you can play in the next game tomorrow morning. You were a real trooper while packing up Gran's house. She convinced your mom and me to make the detour to Chicago so that you can help your softball team. We called Coach Todd and he talked to the tournament officials. They're allowing you to finish the tournament in Mya's place. In fact, there are a few young ladies who want to welcome you."

Screams and cheers filled the lobby of the hotel. It was my team. They were happy to see me, and I was equally excited to see them.

"I'll leave you all to get caught up and do whatever softball girls do," dad said, handing me my suitcase. "We'll see you in the morning, D.J."

"Daddy," I stopped him. "Thank you so much. Tell mama and Gran thanks as well. I won't let you all down."

"I know you won't. Go Diamond Dolls!"

For the next forty-five minutes, Coach Todd and the team filled me in on what we're up against with the team we're playing next, and our plan of action.

"I'm so glad you're here, D.J.," London said as we huddled. "I don't know if I can fill your shoes or your position."

"I'm glad to be here. You'll do fine, London; don't forget you're starting the game. I'm your backup."

"Alright, ladies. It's time to call it a night. No

parties in your rooms. It's lights out. We have to go to work tomorrow. And D.J., we are glad to have you with us. Put in work on three. One. Two. Three."

"PUT IN WORK!" filled the lobby.

I DON'T KNOW if it's because I slept the entire ride yesterday; or that I'm excited, nervous, and anxious about the game, but it was tough to fall asleep last night. When sleep did finally show up, I played the upcoming game in my dreams all night. We won and lost, won and lost. One thing for sure, the hotel's bed was a lot better than the couch I recently slept on at Gran's.

Up early before everyone else, I got ready and was out of the way. While I waited for my teammates to get dressed, I'm getting game ready. Nelly's *Heart of a Champion* is playing in my ears, and I'm channeling all the energy, enthusiasm, and grit I can to be prepared to face our opponents this morning. It's safe to say that I'm in my zone. So much so, I didn't realize it's time to leave.

"D.J., snap out of it. It's time to head out," Jade was nose-to-nose with me. "Come on. Everyone else is in the elevator."

Everyone on our team takes softball seriously, and winning is a big part of it. Although we don't always win every game, we go into every game believing we will win, no matter who we're playing. Before a game, there is no laughing and playing. We have to be mentally prepared to go to work. On the ride to the ballpark, the van is quiet and everyone is in their own zone, mentally preparing for the game.

"Okay, we've arrived. Before we get off the van, I'd like to say something. First, you all are one helluva group of young ladies, and I'm proud to be your coach. Not if, but when we win this game, we'll be back in the winner's bracket. That means there will be a second game this afternoon. I plan to start the second string, saving the first string as much as I can for this afternoon. London, you're up first at shortstop."

"But, coach," London started.

"You've got this. Confidence is key, " I interrupted. "And, I have your back."

London nodded. Everyone grabbed their bat bags and walked toward the ballpark, with confidence, and ready to put in work.

No matter how laser-focused on the game I tried to stay, my mind kept going back to Gran. Because of her, I had to miss the tournament. And because of her, I'm able to compete in the tournament with my team.

Taking to the field to warm up, we are welcomed with cheers from the entire stand behind our dugout. Looking into the crowd, I spotted my family. Gran is cheering the loudest and waving her hands like she's signaling SOS for a passing airplane. A couple of years ago, that would have embarrassed me to no end. But now, I love it. I see where mama gets it from, it has been a very long time since Gran has seen me play. I'm glad she's here.

"Let's play ball," the announcer growls over the speaker after the national anthem.

"Batting first for the Diamond Dolls is number nine, Zoe," is announced over the speakers. We're the visitors and first at bat.

Zoe stands in the batter's box and swings a couple of times then walks to home plate. Stepping to the plate, she plants her feet, points to center field with her bat, then positions it over her shoulder. The crowd goes wild. Zoe is good for making you think she's going to send the ball one way, but sends it ripping in a totally different direction.

And she swings.

"Striiiike," the umpire bellows.

"This dugout is too quiet," Stormy yells.

Zoe hits the bottom of her cleats with the bat as if she's knocking the dirt off her shoes, then positions the bat over her shoulder again to show she's ready. The pitcher released the ball, and Zoe made contact, sending a line drive past third base right into left field. Before the ball could be thrown back to infield, Zoe was on second base. Coach Todd signaled her to stop and stay where she was.

Next up to bat were Piper and Emory. Three pitches, three strikes, and they were both out. We're looking at two outs and a man on second. Up to bat next is Big Mac. Coach sends her a couple of signals; she nods and swings on the first pitch. It's a strike.

"Run, run, run!" Coach yells and signals to Zoe. The catcher dropped the ball, giving Zoe a chance to steal to third base. When she makes it to third base, Zoe leans back with her hands in the air and revs up her imaginary motorcycle. The dugout cheers louder.

Zoe, we miss you

Come home

Come home

Zoe, we miss you

Zoe, we miss you

Come home

Come home

. . .

COACH SENDS Big Mac another signal, and she nods again. The pitch is thrown, she bunts and takes off for first base. Zoe makes it home and Big Mac is put out at first base. She laid down the sacrifice so that Zoe could score. Then we take to the field.

The girls run out on the field and I can tell London is nervous. We make eye contact and I make a heart with my hands and put it to my chest and mouth, 'Heart of a Champion.' The infield players get in the ready position, and with their gloves, tap the ground three times, and we all yell. "Three up. Three down."

Rosie throws fire over the plate.

"Striiiike," the umpire roars and our dugout erupts.

Rosie feeds off of our energy and throws a second strike, and then a third. The stands behind us are cheering as the girls run off the field. Our opponents, *Battitudes*, showed no sign of emotion. They headed back outfield looking as if they are prepared to go to war.

"Calm down, ladies," Coach Todd warned. "That was just the first inning. You know how wrong or right things can go from here. Check out your opponents, they're cool as cucumbers. Let's keep it together and not celebrate prematurely. D.J., you're up next to bat."

Grabbing a helmet and my bat, I meet Jade at the door of the dugout where we have our ritual handshake before either of us bats the first time of the game. As I approach home plate, I think I hear my name and look into the stands. Gran is standing and waving.

"Smack that ball, D.J.," Gran yells with her arms waving.

Did I just hear what I thought I heard? Surely, Gran did not just call me D.J. I had to focus real hard to keep from laughing. Looking over my shoulder, I get of glimpse of the coach's signal and nod. I hear my team in the dugout and tune them out. It's only me, the pitcher, and the catcher. She winds her pitch, in what seems like slow motion and releases a curveball. The tip of my bat gets only a piece of the ball.

The pitcher smiles and winks at me, but I'm laser-focused. She winds her pitch and throws it again, and I don't bite.

"Ball," the umpire calls.

"Way to watch it. Way to, way to watch it," Jade yells.

. . .

READJUSTING MY STANCE, I wait for the next pitch. I make contact, a line drive right past third base. That seems to be a weak spot, coach signaled me to test it. It was good enough for me to get to second base. I'm not as fast as Zoe, but I'm quick. Today, the idea of getting back into the winner's bracket has me motivated to make an extra effort.

IT DIDN'T TAKE LONG for seven innings to come and go. We came out on top.

"CONGRATULATIONS, Diamond Dolls, you pulled it off. We're on our way to the winner's bracket this afternoon. I'm not going to lie, this next game will be a true fight to the finish."

9

Our families met the team in the stands behind the dugout, where there were hugs and cheers. Looking around, my family consisted of only J.P.

"There's a problem," J.P. said as I approached him.

"Problem? What kind of problem? Where is everyone else?"

"We can't find Gran. She left to use the bathroom and didn't come back. Mama, daddy, J.R. and the police are looking for her."

"The police? Do they think something happened to her? Come on. We have to help look for her."

"Wait, mama said to stay put. When they find

her, she will call? D.J., they will find Gran, won't they?"

"Of course, they will. Gran probably started talking to someone and lost track of time. You know she'll start a conversation with anyone about anything." I tried to reassure my brother. But I was more nervous than I let on.

"Is everything okay?" Coach Todd asked.

"Yes. My parents are looking for my Gran. Do you mind if I stay behind with my family untill they find her?"

"We will all wait with you," Coach said, turning to the team. "We're a team; we play together and wait together."

Coach Todd had no idea how that made me feel. Our team is more than a team, we're an extended family and I love that about us.

An announcement came over the speakers. "Excuse me, folks. A family is looking for an older lady. Her name is Ophelia Bergeron. She's wearing blue pants, a white T-shirt with a yellow softball."

That announcement sent chills all over my body with the realization that Gran is missing. I was trying my best to hold it together for J.P. If I showed my true feelings, he'd be more afraid.

It's been more than five minutes and J.P.'s phone

has been silent. Sitting and waiting is not helping me at all. I feel the anxiety rising and taking control. I try to suppress it, but it has more control over me than I have over it.

"I'll be right back," I screamed, jumping up from my seat and running away to help find Gran.

"D.J. mama said stay," I heard J.P. shouting.

There was no way I could sit while the police looked for Gran. I ran around looking in both men and women's bathrooms alike.

"Excuse me, can I help you? You do know this is a men's bathroom," an elderly gentleman asked. "Are you running from someone? Are you okay?"

"I'm looking for my Gran. Have you seen my Gran?"

"She's not here," he answered. "Are you sure you're okay? There are police around that can protect you from whatever you're running from."

"I'm looking for my Gran," I shouted, holding back tears and running to find the next bathroom.

"Excuse me."

I'm so sorry," I said because I bumped into a few people on the walk and under the stands.

"Watch where you're going," a guy yelled when I made him spill his drink.

I had no time to stop and apologize. At this point,

I don't know if Gran needed me to find her, as much as I needed to find Gran. Trying not to think, but crazy thoughts were creeping into my head.

"Let me go. Let me go," I demanded, trying to break free.

"Calm down," J.R. behind me as I struggled to get out of his grip. "We found Gran. Why didn't you stay put like J.P. told you? Everyone but you are at the infirmary near the main entrance."

Just as he said, my family and the entire team, along with their families, were at the infirmary.

"Gran, are you okay?" I asked, throwing my arms around her neck and holding her tight.

"I'm fine, D.J. I don't know why everyone is fussing. I just got a little turned around and didn't know how to get back to where we were sitting. All this fuss of taking my temperature, blood pressure, and sugar is not necessary."

"Since you won't let us take you to the hospital, we at least want you to be looked at here by the EMT's. The people who found you said you were asking how to get back to Chester Hill. You're a long way from home, Gran," daddy said.

Immediately, I thought about the conversation mama and I had about Gran coming to live with us. She said Gran hadn't been herself lately.

"Gran, we just need to know that you're okay," I rubbed her arm. "Did I hear you call me D.J. during the game?"

"Yes, I did. I thought I would try it on for size," Gran smiled. "Thank you all. I am just a little hot and could stand a nice cold drink and a nap. Do you think it would be okay if I went back to the hotel to take a nap?"

"That would be a good idea," the EMT responded. "We're done here. If there are any other problems, make sure to get her to the nearest ER and do a follow-up with her doctor."

My family left for the hotel and I stayed with the team. With Gran safe, I can concentrate on the next game. Now, more than ever, it's important to get my head in the game.

"I HAVE NEWS," Coach Todd came into our team meeting. "I just learned that if we win this next game, we will play for the tournament championship. Winning the last game gave us a great position in the brackets."

"Are you saying what I think you're saying, coach?" Reese said in her booming voice. I've often wondered if she's partially deaf. Her normal, inside voice is an eight when she's excited, it's a fourteen.

"That depends on what you're thinking," Coach Todd responds and we all laugh.

"The top three teams make it to the National Championship tournament at Disney World in Florida. Win or lose, do we go to Florida?" Reese asked.

"Reese, I would say you're thinking is right," Coach confirmed. "But before you start cheering, I want to make something clear. We're playing to be number one, not two or three. Do I make myself clear?"

"Yes, coach," we all agreed in unison.

"I can't hear you?"

"Yes, coach," we shouted.

"Good. I don't want to see any celebrating until it's all over. Block Florida from your minds, focus, and let's play, Diamond Dolls. Gather your things. It's time to warm up. I forgot to mention that we're playing the same team that sent us to the loser's bracket. Put in work on three."

As we warm up, I try to stay focused and not think about that bomb coach dropped on us. We have to face the same team that beat us initially. We can't let that change anything. The Diamond Dolls have what it takes to take them down.

The stands were starting to fill up with fans and other teams. We can't have our devices on the field while we're warming up, so I'm going through my playlist in my head. The only song I'm hearing is Beyoncé's *Ring The Alarm*. I'm nodding to the music in my head and going through our warmup drills.

Jade signals for me to run our drill for a double play, but I shake it off. Instead, I just throw the ball. And she signals again. I look past her and act like I didn't see it, and throw her a ground ball instead.

"I thought you said you were okay," Jade asked as she approached.

"I am okay, just trying to stay laser-focused."

The team we are about to play is good, and it will be much tougher than the last game. We're the visiting team again since we're returning to the winner's bracket. Although it may feel like we're the underdog, coach says we're going to use batting first to our advantage.

Leaving the field so our opponents can warm-up, I couldn't help myself. I looked in the stands for my family, wondering if Gran would be okay enough to make it back out to the game. Scanning the stands quickly before the coach catches me looking, I couldn't find my family in the growing crowd of fans and spectators.

We head to the ladies room to freshen up before the game. Some of us reapply eye shadow, lip gloss or fix our bows in our hair. One of the reasons we're named Diamond Dolls, though we're a heavy-hitting, hard-playing, get down and dirty softball team, we're girly. We show up to every game dolled up, just in our softball uniforms.

10

———

"Coach, I have something to say, if I may," I break the silence of our dugout and everyone stops to look at me.

"Be my guest," Coach Todd nods.

"Win, lose, or draw, Dolls we're heading to Disney World in Orlando, Florida to play in the national tournament," I start. "That's weeks away. Right here and right now, our mission is to not lose to the same team twice. Let's make some noise and kick some butt. Who's with me? Put in work on three."

"Play ball!" the umpire yelled.

It looks like it's going to be a long game. We were up to bat first, and it was three up and three down. We returned the favor. That went on for three innings. No one has gotten a hit or made it to first base. We knew this was going to be a tough game and The Hit Squad is bringing the heat. The Diamond Dolls are matching their energy and fire.

Every fly ball caught, ground balls fielded and slung to first putting the batter out, strikeouts and no walks. Both teams are bringing their best game and neither one is giving up a run.

"Okay, ladies. It's time to make something shake," coach says as we run to the dugout to prepare for the fourth inning. "We need to score and score in this inning. Big Mac, make it happen."

McKenzie, being up to bat first this inning, was just what we needed to change the direction of the game. She hit it, ripped it, and sent it sailing to score the board.

"And that looks like a homerun for number eight, McKenzie 'Big Mac' of the Diamond Dolls. Wake up, folks. We finally have some action in this ball game," the announcer says over the speaker.

That was just the jolt we needed. We had two more runs that inning, bringing it to three, and we are stoked. Maybe a little too much for Coach Todd's liking.

"Listen, we're in this ball game, but we haven't won. I need you to stay focused on the task at hand;

playing and winning this game. No celebrating untill the end," Coach Todd reminded us. "As we head back out, keep in mind the other team is hungry for a win as well. Let's go to work."

And just like that, The Hit Squad scores and we end the inning three to two, and we're up.

The sixth inning was a no score for both teams. Jules, Piper, and I were all able to get on base this inning, but we just could not pull off a run. It was important to keep our lead moving into the sixth inning if we're going to win this game.

"The pressure is on ladies. Here's the deal. We have to score this inning, or we'll have to play defense as you've never played to keep them from scoring. Dig deep and give me all you got. This is the last inning."

Our turn up to bat did not produce a run. Not a single run. Frustrated, a little nervous, and a lot exhausted, we take the field to play the defense of our lives. Our fans send us out with cheers. Too bad that energy from the fans couldn't fuel us. We needed it.

Rosie steps to the plate and the cheers continue.
Hubba, hubba, hubba,
Ding-a-ling-a-ling,
Our pitchers got an arm like a pitching machine!

The batter hits Rosie's first pitch of the inning, sending a line drive straight past Jules on third base. Lydia, in left field, was all over it, scooping it up and throwing it to me at shortstop. I was ready to tag the runner. She smiled and knew to stay put on second base. Adrenaline kicked in, and we all seemed to perk up.

"Throw that fire," Stormy yelled from second base.

And the batter hit a ground ball, straight to me. I scooped it up, tagged the runner as she was trying to make her way to third base. Jade was in position and I slung past Rosie, in what seemed like slow motion. Jade caught it! Jade freakin caught it! For the very first time, when it counted, Jade and I made the connection for a double play!

I know coach said not to celebrate, but I couldn't help it. It felt like we just won the game. We were one out from winning. Rosie walked the next two batters, and the following two brought in a runner each.

"That's the ball game," the umpire shouted.

The Diamond Dolls lose to The Hit Squad by one. We line up to shake hands and their coach stops Jade and me.

"Great game. You two are great players and had

me worried about this game. I look forward to seeing the two of you play again in the future."

Although we had just lost this game, I was very excited. Actually, I was more than excited, but I can't think of the appropriate word at this point. Jade and I pulled off a double play. We've worked on it, attempted it in game situations, and even discussed it. Coach Todd said it was all about timing, we couldn't overthink it, and one day, things would just click. Today was that day. Playing it back constantly over in my head, I don't know how it clicked. I wasn't thinking about it. Jade wasn't thinking about it. We read each other and I threw the ball. The rest is history.

"GRAN, you will never guess what happened today," I rushed in and jumped on the bed right next to her.

"Well, let me guess. With that smile, I imagine you all won,"' Gran sat up in the bed to look at me.

"No, we lost," I shrugged, "But."

"What. Wait a minute. That smile and all of this excitement and you say you all lost. I have to hear this. Do tell."

I jumped off the bed to demonstrate fully.

"So, I was at shortstop right, in the ready position. There was a runner on second," I started showing Gran my stance. "The batter hit a ground ball right to me. I scooped it up in my glove, tagged the runner who thought she was going to get by me. Without hesitation, I shot the ball on a straight line to Jade. And Gran, she caught it, putting the runner out at first."

"What!" Gran shouted. "You and Jade pulled off a"

"Double play!" We screamed in concert.

"The entire hotel can hear you two," J.R. walked into our room. "What's all the bedlam about?"

"Oh, no," Daddy laughed. "The noise level must be pretty bad; J.R. is using his fifty-dollar words."

"D.J. was just demonstrating her, "Gran started.

"Double play," I finished. "I wonder if anyone caught that on video. I'd love to see that over and over and over again."

"If I'm not mistaking, the tournament had someone recording. I'll check on it," daddy said.

"This calls for a celebration," Gran smiled. "I'm up to it."

Gran had given us a pretty good scare earlier. She's trying her best to act like she's okay. Every once in a while, I catch her zoned out and staring into space. Instead of calling her out, I just rub her arm to bring her back from wherever she is in her head. I'm not the only one to notice. I caught mama and daddy both whispering and watching Gran. Maybe they're whispering about whatever it is going on with her and why mama says she's not herself.

11

―――――

"Knock, knock. Do you mind if I come in and hang out with you for a little while?" I asked, standing in the doorway of what used to be my bedroom but now Gran's. "What are you doing?"

"Sure, come on in. I could use the company. I'm just sitting here looking out the window and enjoying a little bird watching. This window gives the perfect view of the pear tree."

"I've always enjoyed watching the birds and squirrels play in that tree as well. I can sit for hours just looking out this window. If you look over to the far right, you can see a nest."

"Yes, there it is. I wonder what kind of bird built that little nest?"

"A hummingbird. I once watched it as the mama bird flew back and forth, feeding her babies. I had a clear view of their nest all summer long. I don't know if it's the same bird, but it's the same species that makes a nest in that tree every year. Daddy has a pair of binoculars you can use that will give you a closer look. It's something amazing to see."

"I'd love that. Now tell me, what's going on with your hair? It looks like birds have been playing in it," Gran laughed.

"Aww, Gran. It's not that bad, is it?" I laughed with her. "I was trying something new and this is the result. Can you help me and braid my hair?"

"I'd love to. It's been a minute since I've braided anyone's hair, but I'm sure I haven't forgotten how to. Hand me that can of oil on the dresser. We must start with a good scalp oiling. Grab a few pillows and have a seat over here in front of me."

Gran parted my hair and applied the oil on my scalp and massaging it in. My eyes rolled back in my head. It had been so long since I had my scalp oiled and massaged like this.

"That feels so good, Gran. What is that?" I asked.

"It's an old family recipe. We've always just called it Harper's hair grower. My cousin, Harper's hair was in a bad way with bald patches. My grandmother,

Daisy, though a midwife, was a Jill of all trades. She made up an oil for Harper's hair. And that child's hair took off and grew like weeds. The recipe has been in our family for years. Every once in a while, I make up a batch for myself so that I don't forget how to make it."

"Can I ask you something, Gran?" I ask, still enjoying her hands in my head.

"Of course. That is if you don't fall asleep first. When you were a little girl, oiling your scalp would put you to sleep when nothing else would."

"It's very relaxing," I tell her. "You got lost in Chicago, at the softball game. What happened? What I want to know is if you are okay?"

"Can I share something with you and be totally honest?"

"Uh-hunh. Sure you can, Gran," I wanted to turn around to look at her. Instead, I stayed put and let her continue to talk and oil my scalp. I was afraid she would make clam up.

"My intention was to go to the bathroom and come right back. I was capable of doing so. But somewhere along the way of returning to my seat, something happened. I can't explain it. I just could not remember which way to go. Things got foggy. It's what my doctor calls disorientation. A young man tried to help me, but I don't know if he confused me more, or I confused him. So, I told him I saw my family and he left me there. I wandered around a little while longer in the sun and got hot, agitated, and more confused.

"My doctor says I'm in the first stages of dementia. Since being diagnosed almost a year ago, I've had a few episodes. Most recently, I couldn't find my way home after leaving the church. They said I drove around for hours. If Uncle Pete had not stopped by to check on me and realized I wasn't home, who knows what would have happened? His brother-in-law, who is a deputy sheriff, found me. I was two miles away from home and couldn't find my way.

After that, you're mama thought it would be better to be with you all instead of bumping around Chester Hill by myself. So, here I am."

"Are you scared? I mean, about losing your memory?"

"I'd be lying if I said no. What scares me the most is forgetting my life, your granddaddy, and my children. I'm most afraid of forgetting you, your brothers, and your cousins. When I was a girl, I watched as my own grandmother forgot everyone that loved her. I never imagined that it would be me one day.

I feel like I'm running out of time. There was so much I wanted to teach you all and tell you about our family; where they came from and who they were. You must know these things. If we don't talk about them with our young people, they cease to exist. All of that information goes to the grave with us."

"I have an idea, Gran. We learned about heritage projects in my history class. It's where we record your family history in a book, video, or audio recording to share and pass on. We should do videos," I explain.

"That's a great idea," Gran lit up. "Our family can have these videos for generations to come. It might even be helpful to help me remember things when I start to forget. You can even continue this when you have a family of your own."

Our heritage project started with interviews. I set up an old cell phone to record videos. For the next several days after dinner, Gran and I sat on the patio when it cooled off outside. It was very informal, just me and Gran talking like good girlfriends.

We talked about things we had already discussed, like Chester Hill, granddaddy, her parents, the old clock, and other things she had not previously shared with me. I had no idea Gran is a twin. She is a card-carrying member of the NAACP, and she played softball.

"No way. You played softball?" I couldn't believe it.

"Yes, I did, and I was good too. First base," Gran nodded with a big smile.

Our sessions were so much fun, and we even gained an audience. Mama was first, then daddy and the boys would join us on the patio. Once we recorded during dinner. That night, we had tacos. I was in disbelief that Gran had never cooked tacos.

One of my favorite sessions had to be the evening we sat on the patio and shelled peas. I came in from softball practice, and there Gran was with several bushel baskets around her feet.

"There you are, come on out here and join me," Gran extended the invitation.

"What in the world are you doing, Gran?" I asked.

"What does it look like I'm doing? I'm shelling purple hull peas."

"You do know you can buy peas already shelled and frozen at the grocery store, right?"

"And why would I do that when I can shell my own fresh peas and freeze them myself. Over there is your pan. You have to catch up. I'm way ahead of you."

Grabbing my phone and tripod, I set up and started shelling peas per her instructions.

"The peas go in your pan, not on the ground," Gran laughed. "Look here. This is how you shell peas. Instead of pulling either side apart and peas flying everywhere. Hold it in your left hand, and with your right thumb press on the inside seam just hard enough to open it. Once your thumb is inside, simply slide it down, pushing the peas out of the pod and into your pan."

"Like this?" I demonstrated.

"Not exactly, but you'll get the hang of it by the time we finish."

"What's wrong with your thumb?" I asked.

"Nothing is wrong with my thumb," Gran laughed. "After shelling purple hull peas for a while, your thumb turns purple."

"Cool. I want a purple thumb too."

"Then you'd better get busy."

We laughed and talked, untill we both forgot the camera was recording.

"Why are you smiling and looking at me like that?" I asked.

"I'm just enjoying the time we're spending together, D.J.," Gran said.

"It reminds me of the time I spent with my grandmother shelling peas, enjoying time doing everything and nothing. We spent hours on her porch swing. I hadn't thought about that swing in years. I always said I would get one for my porch, but I never did. My mawmaw taught me so much."

12

———

Today is the day. Gran and I were finally getting around to making her infamous fried pies, as she promised. Gran collects all the ingredients while I set up the camera. This time, things are a little different. Okay, a lot different. I was in denial and didn't want to admit. Gran couldn't concentrate and seemed a little agitated.

"What kind of fried pies are we making today, Gran?" I asked to get things going and to calm her down a little.

"Fried pies. Yes, we're making fried pies," Gran repeated.

"It looks like apple, my favorite," I try to help her out.

"Call Uncle Pete and tell him to come on over. I

have some work I need him to do before it gets cold," Gran turns to me and says with urgency and seriousness on her face.

At first, I just stand there with my eyes wide open, like a deer stuck in the headlights. I didn't know what to do. I'm standing there looking at Gran, looking at me, looking at her, and then it hit me. She's having an episode. I was on the verge of freaking out because I had never seen her like this and I had no clue what to do.

Eventually, the smoke alarm went off. The oil we were heating to fry the pies was starting to burn. Mama and daddy both came running.

"What's happening?" Mama yelled.

"Turn it off, D.J." Daddy said. "Turn off the pot."

"Something's wrong with Gran. I think she's having an episode," I whispered to mama, never turning back to the stove to turn off the smoking pot of oil.

Daddy went to the stove, and mama took Gran by the hand and lead her to the den and sat her down. I followed right behind them like a little puppy. Gran continued to explain that she had some work for Uncle Pete, and she wanted it done soon before the cold weather set in.

"Yes, ma'am," mama agreed. "I'll call him in just a

few minutes and get him right over here. First, Gran, I need to ask you a question. Where are we right now?"

"That's a dumb question. Are you going to call Uncle Pete, or do I have to get him on the phone myself?"

Then there was nothing. Gran just stopped talking and stared into space. I didn't know what to do, so I just sat there watching mama try to bring Gran back from the place she had gone to in her mind.

"I'm pulling the car around," my dad shouted from the kitchen.

"D.J., grab my purse," mama instructed. "We're taking Gran to the emergency room."

"I'm going with you," I finally managed to get a word out.

"I need you to stay home and hold the fort down. Can you do that for me?" Mama asked. "Gran will be okay. We just need to have her checked out to make sure nothing major is going on. We'll call you soon."

I just nodded and did as I was told. By the time I got back downstairs with mama's purse, they were outside in the car. Mama snatched her purse through the window, and daddy sped off. Not knowing what to do or how to feel, I made my way to

Gran's bedroom. Grabbing her robe off the end of the bed, I wrapped myself in it and laid down. In the next few minutes, both of my brothers came in Gran's room where I was. J.P. laid on the bed next to me, while J.R. sat in Gran's rocker. Neither one of us said a word. We comforted each other in silence.

Waking up in the middle of the night, I realized I'm in my bed. I ran down the hall to peep on a a sleeping Gran. A deep sigh of relief escaped my lungs and I am relieved. She looked so comfortable. I had to resist the urge to walk over and straighten her covers and tuck her in. Gran can be a light sleeper and I don't want to wake her. So, I turn to tiptoe back to the room I'm sharing with J.P.

"Geesh, mama, you scared me. Why are you just standing there," I whispered, trying my best not to be loud and wake up the house?

"I was coming to check on Gran as well," she yawned.

"What did the doctor say?" I asked.

"He couldn't be sure, but he thinks she has moved from a mild to moderate stage. We are to see a specialist this week for more conclusive tests and answers." Mama explained. "Remember I told you Gran is not herself? This is part of that."

"Gran has explained to me that she has demen-tia, and about her episodes," I said.

"Yes, and as her condition worsens, there may be more episodes, foggy memory, or times when she will be completely confused as to where she is, and what is going on. It's important that we stay calm and not agitate the situation. The doctors gave her medication to calm her, and she'll probably sleep for a while."

"Thanks, Mama," I tell her, walking toward my bed.

"Thanks for what, D.J.?"

"Thanks for bringing Gran here to live with us, and trusting me enough to tell me the truth about what's going on with her."

"It's important that your daddy and I demon-strate what it means to be good children and care-takers for our parents. One day, when we're old, you'll know what to do and take good care of us," mama confides.

"Mama, I'll always take care of you and daddy. Good night, or morning."

WHILE GRAN SLEEPS off the medicine they gave her in the ER, daddy has gone to work, and mama is working from home. J.P. is at the Boys and Girls Club, and who knows about J.R. I use this time to start editing the videos Gran and I have recorded so far. I want to have something to show Gran soon. I did a little research on my own about dementia. If she's already moving into the next stage, who knows how long it will be before she remembers less and less. I want to show her who she is and jog her memory. But there is so much more we wanted to discuss and record.

Every twenty minutes or so, I peep in on Gran. She's still lying on her left side with her left hand under her head, and her right arm is covering her face. Gran has not moved at all. I want her to wake up so that we can talk, and I know that she's okay.

Standing in the doorway, I remember Mrs. Connaway, our Home Economics teacher saying, "A watched egg won't boil." And I guess, neither will a watched sleeping Gran awake.

I go back to editing our video.

The notifications of my cell phone start making themselves known. It's either Jade or Stormy.

Jade: Hey D.J. Would you like to ride to practice with us, and get ice cream afterward?

My mom says she wants to take the dynamic duo out for a treat.

Me: Tell your mom thanks, but I'll have to take a rain check. I won't be going to practice

today. Gran had an episode last night, and I don't want to leave her. She might need me when she wakes up.

Jade: I know how much you love ice cream, but I know you love your Gran more. Hoping

she'll be okay. TTYL

Staying behind has more to do with needing to see Gran, instead of her needing me. The idea of her one day forgetting me has me feeling some kind of way. In my mind, if I am there for her and always around, she won't forget me. It's mostly wishful thinking. In the back of my mind, I know she can't pick and choose who and what she remembers. But if, by the off chance of me being there in her face more will make a difference, I'm going to do so. My face will be the first face she sees when she wakes up.

13

"Well, hello, sleepyhead," I greet Gran when she finally wakes up. Just like I planned, mine was the first face she saw.

"What time is it?" She asked while stretching and yawning. "I feel like I've been asleep for two days.

"It's two fifteen in the afternoon," I tell her.

"It is not. You have got to be kidding. Tell me you're just joking with me," Gran says in disbelief.

"No, ma'am," I assure Gran. "I am not kidding."

"You mean to tell me I've slept through all of my shows? Why didn't someone wake me up? I'm not going to be able to go to sleep tonight."

"I thought I heard your voice. How did you rest?" Mama said, joining us.

"Rest. Is that what you call it?" Gran scoffed. "I was so doped up. It was more of an induced coma than rest. I didn't dream or nothing."

"And you did not move at all," I added. "You usually toss and turn. But you stayed in the same position."

"It's time I get out of this bed. I've got things to do," Gran said, attempting to put her feet on the floor. "Oooo, not so fast, Ophelia."

"Are you okay?" Mama asked.

"Just a woozy feeling. Maybe I should stay put for a little while longer," Gran sunk back into the bed. "Do you think I can have a cup of tea with a couple of those blackberry scones I made the other day?"

"Of course, you can. Your wish is my command," I said, hurrying to make my way to the kitchen.

"And I want sugar cubes instead of granulated sugar," she said just before I walked out of the door.

Gran taking sugar cubes in her tea is one of those things that she got from her grandmother and continued to use them to keep her memory alive. It blew her mind to find out there are flavored sugar cubes. She had mama buy as many different flavors as she could find.

As I steep Gran's tea, I grab a teacup for myself. It's been a long time since I've had a tea party. Now is just as good a time as any. I fix up the tray real nice with the pretty little teapot and scones. I grab the phone and tripod and make my way to Gran's room.

"Are you up for a tea party," I asked as I came through the door.

"A tea party with my favorite girl sounds fun," she said, sitting up on the side of the bed.

"What flavor sugar cubes would you like to try today?" I say trying to imitate an English accent. "We have rose, vanilla, salted caramel, and grapefruit."

"How fancy," she giggles. "I'd like to try the rose. Four, please."

I pour Gran's tea from the cutsie teapot she brought with her from her home and added four rose flavored sugar cubes as requested. Gran stirs her tea until the rock-solid cubes dissolve. I then pour myself a cup and add salted caramel cubes and stir. The clinking of our spoons makes me smile. With my pinky out, I tried to sip my steaming hot tea.

"What are you doing, Gran? Why are you pouring your tea into your saucer? You're supposed to drink from your cup."

Immediately, I started to wonder if Gran was having another episode. She seemed to know what she was doing, but I wasn't sure.

"I'm okay, D.J. I simply remembered something my grandmother used to do. She would pour her tea into her saucer when it was really hot. Then she would blow to cool it, and sip loud, like this."

Gran made the noisiest slurp I ever heard. She slurped louder than J.P.

"Try it," she encouraged.

I pour a little tea into my saucer, blew, and then slurped. We laughed and slurped, rating each other on a scale from one to ten. Gran is much better at slurping than I am, she's a ten every time. We went from slurping to dipping our scones in our tea and enjoying our time.

"You okay?" I ask her. "Do you need to lay down for a while? You're not quite yourself."

"I'm okay. It's the medicine the doctor gave me. It makes me feel weird, a little slow like it takes things a couple of seconds to register," she explained.

"How about I oil your scalp like you did mine?" I ask.

Gran nodded in agreement. I got the tin of Harper's hair grower from her dresser that she used on my scalp, along with her comb. I climbed behind her on the bed, parted her hair, I applied the oil on her scalp and massaged it in; the same way she did mine. Gran started singing.

Poor little Pehlia going to town,
Riding a billy goat, leading a hound.
Hound barked.
Billy goat jumped.
Poor little Phelia straddled a stump.

"What is that you're singing, Gran?" I asked.

"That was one of the songs my mama used to sing to me when she did my hair. Back then, I was so tender-headed until she had to entertain me to keep my mind off her hands in my head. Often, we made up songs. Right now, that's the only song that comes to mind," Gran reminisced.

"When you remember some of those songs, I'd love to hear them," I tell her.

I kept oiling her scalp, and she continued to hum that song over and over, occasionally verbalizing a word here and there. When I finished, I brushed her long, thick silver hair until her head started to bob, heavy from sleep.

"Why don't you take a nap now?" I said, helping her back under the covers and tucking her in.

"Thank you, D.J.," she whispered.

"Daisy, Gran. It's Daisy."

"Is that right?" She smiled.

"Yeah, I'm trying it on for size," I wink at her,

gathering the evidence of our tea party, and heading out the door.

14

———

Softball has always been my go-to for an escape from real life. Today's game was just that. I didn't think about anything but the ball, bat, and our opponents.

We have several more weeks until the softball tournament at Disney World, and several more games between now and then. There are more people at today's game in the stands cheering us on than usual.

"Hey, coach. Where did all these people come from," Jules asked during our warm-up?

"I don't ever remember this many people coming out to our games," Piper added.

"The word is out about the Diamond Dolls," Coach Todd said proudly.

"Whatdaya mean the word is out?" I asked.

"There was a really nice and rather large article in yesterday's newspaper about the Super Summer Showdown in Chicago," coach said.

"But we didn't win," Jules scoffed, kicking up dirt.

"No, we may not have won, but we finished third and made the Disney tournament. That is a big deal. You ladies are a big deal," coach explained.

"Alright team, we have a hometown crowd, let's give 'em a show," I said. "Put in work on three. One, two, three."

"Put in work," we all chant.

Being the home team, we took the field first. Every out we made, there were cheers and the crowd joined in with the dugout chants. When we were up to bat, they cheered even louder.

"I could get used to this level of fan support," Rosie said, warming up her pitching arm.

In the third inning, Jade and I pulled it off again. There were runners on first and second bases, and a batter at the plate. Jade gave me a nod and I returned the gesture with a double punch to my glove.

The batter hit the ball straight toward Jade at first base. She touched first base and threw the ball to me. I tagged the runner, who was attempting to run back to second. Another double play! The crowd went wild, chanting our names. Yes, I can surely get used to this type of fan support.

I look to the stands where daddy and my brothers were waving and cheering. Mama stayed home with Gran. Since her trip to the hospital, she's been sleeping a lot more. Although she said she felt fine and wanted to attend my game, mama thought it was best to stay home this time.

We won eight to five over the Power Drivers. These girls we play against have been playing softball as long as we have and are exceptional. Coach reminds us often that our advantage is our chemistry. After shaking hands with the other team, fans lined up along the fence to get our autographs and take pictures with us. Most of my teammates were excited about the attention. I'm not shy at all, but it kind of made me uneasy. I just wanted to sneak off, but the coach waved me over.

"D.J., I'd like for you to meet Shiloh," He introduced me to a little girl wearing her glove and the biggest brown eyes I'd ever seen.

"Well, hello, Shiloh, I'm D.J.," I said, kneeling to be eye to eye with her.

"I'm Shiloh and I'm six years old. One day, I'm going to play shortstop and make double plays like you. Can you sign my ball?" she said, pulling a soft-ball out of her glove.

"Sure, I'd love to," I said, reaching for Coach Todd's pen.

I signed the ball and stepped back a few paces and tossed the ball into her glove.

"Thanks," she smiled. "Thanks so much."

That was my cue. I turned to walk to the dugout and grab my bat and bag.

"See you all at the pool party later," Coach Todd yelled out the reminder as daddy, the boys and I were headed out of the park gate.

"Sounds like fun, D.J. You've gotta go," Daddy nudged. "You need to get out some. You've been home with Gran since we made it back from Chicago."

Shrugging my shoulders, I wasn't committing either way. I'll just have to see what happens.

"It's about time you made it," Jules said as I walked toward my teammates. "I was beginning to think you weren't coming."

"Wow, this party is nice," I said, admiring everything from the decorations, to the food, and the D.J. playing music in the corner.

"Can I have your autograph?" A guy walks up with a newspaper and pen. "And while you're at it, your phone number too."

Taking the newspaper, I see it's the article Coach Todd told us about earlier. What he didn't mention was the picture of the team along with a picture of me throwing the ball to Jade for the infamous double play. I stood there for a second, just looking at the picture. Suppressing a giggle and the urge to smile, I quickly signed the paper and handed it back to Jonah Payne.

Wait, Jonah Payne wanted my autograph. Now I'm also trying to tame the butterflies that are leaping, twirling, and fluttering in my stomach. What I couldn't hide was the flush of red that started at my neck and covered my face. After giving him back the paper, he didn't leave, he just stood there and struck up a conversation.

"Why don't you ever hang out at the pool?" He asked. "You can swim, can't you?"

"Of course, I can swim. Coach's number one rule during the softball season is no swimming. It takes all of your energy in your legs. And during the season, we always have a game."

What I didn't explain was the actual extent of my swimming is a crawl, which looks more like a doggie paddle. One he'll never get to see.

"If we can't go swimming, where can I take the famous D.J. out on a date?" Jonah asked.

"Did I miss something?" I laughed. There was not even an ask. I handed him his pen and walked away to join Jade at the drink cooler. He returned to the group of his friends showing them the newspaper with my autograph and phone number.

"Did you just give Jonah your phone number?" Jade asked.

"I did not. I gave him J.R.'s number."

We both laughed so hard and made our way back to our teammates at the photo booth.

The rest of the evening, the team signed newspapers for *friends of the team*. That's what coach calls them. Mama says they're more like a booster club.

15

Coming in from the pool party, J.R. and I came through the garage into the kitchen where the family was sitting with smiling faces and the biggest cupcake I've ever seen.

"What's all of this? And what are we celebrating?" I ask.

"We are celebrating you, our very own celebrity," daddy said, handing me a framed copy of the article in yesterday's paper.

"Thank you. Thank you. Thank you all so much," I said in my goofy voice and bowing to each of my family members. "And is this cupcake for me too? It's big enough for all of us to take a bite."

"Come on in the den," J.P. pulled on my arm. "There's more."

"More? What more could there be?" I asked.

Daddy turned on the TV and it was the infamous double play from the Summer Softball Showdown.

"Oh-M-Geeee, someone edited the video! I love it. The music and effects are amazing. I can't wait to show Jade. I might even upload it to my social media accounts. It's sure to go viral. And I have something to share with you all."

I ran to my room to get my computer and was back in a flash.

"This past year, I learned about heritage projects in our African American History class. Gran and I created our very own video. Behold."

I sat and watched my family as they watched the video I created with interviews of Gran, interactions with each one of us, and pictures from the few old photo albums she brought with her. Daddy and the boys smiled; they're always very easy to read. Mama is always emotional; she cries watching mushy commercials. She sat clutching her nonexistent pearls with tears streaming down her face. I was more concerned with how Gran would react to the video. Would she approve?

When the video ended, everyone applauded, everyone except Gran. I held my breath.

"Daisy," Gran started to speak. "I am at a loss for words."

"Oh, no! You didn't like it?" I asked.

"The complete opposite. I loved every minute of it, especially the two of us having tea. You were able to capture the history of our family, along with the fun and love we share. You are a talented storyteller, producer, camera person, and editor. One of these days, you're going to give Miss Ava Duvernay a run for her money. I went to school with a few Duvernays. I wonder if they're related."

"Gran, not everyone with the same last name is related," J.R. laughed, causing all of us to follow in belly-aching laughs.

It felt so good to be surrounded by my family, laughing at literally nothing. But the thought did creep into my mind that one day, I'll look back on this day and wish for it again.

"WHO'S AT THE DOOR? Are we expecting anyone?" Daddy asked, following the doorbell ringing.

"There is only one way to find out," Mama said, making us laugh all over again.

"Look who I found at the door," Daddy said with Coach Todd following behind him.

"Hey, coach. What's up?" I asked, confused as to why he would show up at our house unannounced, especially after I saw him today at a game and the pool party. "Is something wrong?"

"No, I have good news," he started. "First, let me apologize for just stopping by. Seeing how it's the weekend, I just could not wait until Monday's practice to tell you."

"Tell her what?" Gran interrupted. "Spit it out already while I can still remember it."

"Yes, of course. Right after the pool party, I heard from the national softball tournament commission. They have chosen the players for the all-star game that takes place after the tournament play. You were one of three members of our team selected to play?"

"Wait," I said, trying to wrap my mind around what Coach Todd was saying. "I had no idea I was even being considered for an all-star team. And you said three people from our team made it. Who else?"

"Jade and Rosie also made it. The best part is the three of you are guaranteed to play your position. You see why I was way too excited to sit on this information until Monday evening."

"Wow, coach. I don't know what to say?" I could barely get the words out of my mouth.

"How about starting with you accept," J.R. blurted. "Coach, you are a magician. You shut D.J. down and she has no words."

"Good night I have to make two more stops to share the news," coach said, heading to the door. "And D.J., don't call either one of them. I want to be the one to surprise them."

Excited, stunned, and a little confused, my emotions are all rolled up into one big ball. It's tough not to pick up the phone to call or text Jade or Rosie. We're not just teammates. We're real friends who share everything. Now, I just have to wait until they call me. What do I do while I wait?

Unknown:What's up? What are you up to?

Me:Who is this, and how did you get my number?

Unknown:Remember, you gave me your number at the pool party?

Me: Nope. I didn't give ANYONE my number at the pool party.

Unknown:You're right. You gave me your brother's number, and he gave me yours.

. . .

I DROPPED my phone and looked at it real suspicious as if he can see me reading the text. I made my way to find J.R.

"How could you?" I questioned.

"How could I?" J.R. asked. "I warned you about giving guys my number. The last time, I was texting two days with who I thought was Melody Clark. But you had given my number to Brice Alexander. Why won't you tell them you're not interested?"

"You wouldn't understand," I snapped.

"Try me."

"I'm not confident when it comes to guys. I don't know what to say or do. I just give them your number."

"What? Miss softball confidence herself. I don't believe you."

"Believe it, lover boy. When it comes to guys, I'm awkward. Besides, if I give them your number, I expect you to blow them off for me and I don't have to worry about it."

"One of these days, D.J., you're going to have to deal with boys on you're on. I can't and won't be there to scare them all away. And if I continue to do that, how will you ever find the one for you? Ready or not, Jonah is your opportunity to test the waters. Just know when you need me, I've got your back."

Instead of continuing to go back and forth with J.R., I stuck my tongue out at him and walked off.

"That's big of you," he yelled.

"Thank you. Thank you very much."

My phone buzzed again. I peeked over at it, hoping it was Jade or Rosie. Sliding my phone open really slowly, it was neither of the girls. Instead, it was Jonah again.

Jonah:Hey. You there?

Me:Maybe.

Jonah:Why did you give me your brother's number? You could have just said no.

Me: Do you want the truth?

Jonah:Of course. Honesty is the best policy.

Me:Honestly, I don't know.

Jonah:Really, D.J.?

Me:Yes. I'm not shy, but when it comes to interacting with guys outside of my brothers and friends, I don't know what to say or how to act.

Jonah:Cool, I understand. You can't go wrong, just being you.

Me:I can do that. My friends are calling. I have to take this call.

Jonah: Okay. Good night. Can I text or call you tomorrow?

Me:Yes.

I cannot believe I just agreed to let Jonah text or call me tomorrow. I'm about to answer the call from my friends, but I am not ready to share this with them. Not yet.

16

"Can you believe it?" I screamed, answering the FaceTime call, and seeing both Jade and Rosie. "All three of us made the all-star team!"

"I had no idea we were even in the running," Rosie said.

"Coach Todd told my dad that everyone in that tournament was being considered. He didn't tell us because he didn't want to make us any more nervous than we were. If one of us made it, great. And if we didn't, no problem," Jade said. "And now that the three of us have made it, it's the icing on the cake."

"D.J., I'm so glad you were able to make it to the tournament," Rosie gushed. "Now the three of us are playing in the nationals' all-star game together. This is the absolute best summer ever, especially since the two of you have that double plaything down-pat."

"Yes, a double play kind of summer," I agreed. "When I got home from the pool party, my family surprised me with a little celebration. My dad even had an edited video of the double play at the tournament. And it is fire! I can't wait for you to see it."

"I have to have a copy. I am the other half of that play, you know," Jade laughed.

"But, of course," I said. " I am so glad we get to experience this together."

"Okay, don't start getting mushy on us, D.J.," Rosie said "By the way, how's your Gran? I didn't see her at the game."

"She's okay, I guess. The meds the doctor put her on has her a little zoned out. Do you remember Crawford from third grade? He went from bouncing off the wall to a total zombie. She's not that bad, but something like that. We've had a lot of fun so far making videos and memories that we can look back on."

"OMG, I had forgotten all about Crawford. I felt so sorry for him. He could barely remember his name. I'm a little jealous," Rosie confided. "I never knew either of my grandmothers. The only grandparent I have is Pawpaw Baker, and he's a real jackass. I wish we could trade him in."

"Rosie, you can't say that about your pawpaw. Take it back," Jade fussed. "Even if he is, it has to be some kind of bad juju to say it."

"He's mean, hateful, and a miserable old man. And I will not take it back."

"I'm closer to my dad's mom, Gigi. She comes to visit us, calls and likes to do fun stuff. Martha, my mom's mom, she wants us to call her by her name, says she doesn't like kids. So we only visit when we have to, and she doesn't come to visit at all. My mom says she's the one missing out, not us," Jade said.

"Enough about grandparents," Rosie said. "Let's talk about boys. D.J., Jonah could not stop watching you at the pool party. I would have loved to see his face when he realized you gave him your brother's number."

"Ummm. One, Jonah was not watching me. And two, I don't care about his face when and if he called my brother. He probably isn't even interested in me. He got my number just to impress his boys. Besides, Jonah doesn't like athletes. He's into high-heel wearing, Barbie wannabes."

"Yeah, right. That boy was almost drooling watching you," Rosie laughed. "Tell her, Jade."

"Do we have to do this right now? Okay, I'll play along," Jade said, all dry. "D.J., half the guys there were drooling over you. You act is if you don't care and brush them off. That makes them swoon over you even more. Us watching boys watch you have become the story of our lives."

"Okay, both of you are imaging things. It's been a long day. I'm tired and saying good night. Talk to you guys tomorrow."

That probably would have been the perfect time to tell them about Jonah texting me. But for what? As I said, he's not into athletes, just Barbie wannabes. And the Barbie type, I am not.

Yes, I'm girly, but I'm not an over-the-top primadonna, and he likes them dumb. That's usually the type he goes for, and that is not who I am. Sure, he's handsome and smart, but I do not care. Playing myself is not what's about to happen. Anyway, I don't need distractions, we're preparing for the national tournament and I need my head in the game.

There will probably be college coaches at this tournament scouting players. I want to get on a few of those coaches' radars. That is if I plan to get a full ride to college, between academics and softball.

"Good morning," Mama greets me. "How did you sleep last night?"

"Umm, okay, I guess," I answered.

"Sleeping in is unlike you. I thought maybe you didn't sleep well. You're usually up before everyone else, working out, running, or something. Even as a little child, you've always been an early riser. At one time, it was cute. As you got to the third grade. You started waking everyone else up because you wanted someone to talk to, and that ended the cuteness. You sure you are feeling alright? It is so unlike you to sleep in."

"Yesterday was a long day, but I'm fine. I guess my body needed a little more rest, but I had no idea it's afternoon."

"I left your breakfast in the microwave."

"Thanks, but I'm not exactly hungry either."

"You're sleeping in, and not hungry, call the doctor."

"Really funny. You see my face, don't you?"

My phone buzzes in my hand, and I open it and take a quick look. It's a text from Jonah.

"Distraction," I mumble and lock my phone again.

"*Are you there?*" He texts again.

"*Text back when you get this. I'll be waiting*," Jonah texted a third time.

What is wrong with him? I said he could text me today, not harass me. Not two minutes later, he calls. I ignore it quickly. Now he gets the hint. I don't want to talk to him.

"Someone is blowing you up," mama laughed. "Who are you avoiding?"

"No one and I'm not avoiding them. I'm busy," I said with a sarcastic eye roll.

"Busy, huh?" Mama laughed. "Busy avoiding someone and lying to your mama about it. But, whatever."

"Jonah said, will you text back or return his call. He knows you sent him to voice mail on purpose," J.R. stormed into the kitchen and put it all out there.

"Jonah, huh?" Mama smiled. "Is that Jonah from."

"Mama!" I said, storming out of the kitchen.

"You're leaving your phone."

"You can call him back," I said without thinking.

On second thought, I'd better get my phone before she calls him back for real.

"Thank you. I'll take that," I said, taking the phone from mama's hand.

Why didn't J.R. just tell him I'm not interested?

Instead, he tells me to return his messages. I am so over them both.

"Hey, Gran, I thought I'd find you out here on the patio," I said, taking a seat. "How are you today?"

"I'm feeling more like myself," she smiled. "I'm enjoying sitting out here listening to the birds and watching the bees go from flower to flower. Your mama's patio is the closest thing to my porch and its fancier. If it were not for mosquitoes, I would probably sleep out here. You slept in. All of the excitement of yesterday caught up with you."

"You may be right, Gran. There was a lot of excitement yesterday. And now that you bring it to my attention, I was a little wound up when I got in the bed. With so much on my mind, it was hard to fall asleep."

"The next time you find yourself having trouble falling asleep, try a cup of hot tea," she instructed.

"Gran, is there a tea for everything?" I laughed.

"My grandmother, Daisy would say so. Tea and ginger ale were her go-to for ailments. She had teas for a headache, stomachache, insomnia, cramps, constipation, and acid reflux. Your mama takes medicine for everything. I tried to get her to drink tea. But she swears she doesn't like tea."

"Look what I caught," J.P. said, approaching us on

the patio. "I was up super early to go fishing with my friend Nic, his dad and brothers."

"Oooo, that looks like dinner," Gran said, getting up to take a better look. "That's a good-looking catch."

"We sat on the bank forever being quiet. I almost fell asleep when I finally got a nibble and pulled in this big one right here. After that, the fish were waiting just for us to bait our hooks so they could bite. One after the other, we reeled fish in. Mr. Castle said it was beginner's luck. After each one of us had six fish, we packed it up. He said we should save some for others."

"Grab a spoon, newspaper, and a knife, I'll show you how to clean your fish, then we'll cook your catch of the day for dinner," Gran said.

That was my cue. I was having no parts of cleaning fish or watching the act. I'll wait until it's on my plate.

It had been a while since Jonah's last text or call, or J.R.'s blasting that I call him back. Maybe he finally got the message that I am not interested.

17

"Good afternoon, Diamond Dolls. You all should have received an email of our workout and practice schedules for the next few weeks in preparation for nationals," Coach Todd started the team meeting before practice. "I've also added an assistant coach to take over workouts. This tournament is a new level for us, and we will prepare for it with that in mind. Help me welcome, Coach Ros."

"Welcome, Coach Ros!" we all shouted and waved.

Coach Ross seems intimidating. She's about five-ten with guns for arms that rival that of a bodybuilder. Her eyes are hidden behind dark shades.

She had on a pink visor that matched her pink shorts and pink shoes.

"Hello. I'm looking forward to working with you all," she said. Her voice is just as intimidating as her look. "Today, I will observe you practicing to gauge your strengths and weaknesses. By next practice, I'll have an idea of just where to start with conditioning. I'm asking you to trust the process."

Whenever someone says to trust the process, I know they are about to stick it to me. Jade, Rosie, and I make eye contact. Without saying a word, we communicated our fear of Coach Ros.

"One more thing before we start practice. Let's congratulate D.J., Rosie, and Jade. They will represent our team and our region in the nationals all-star game."

The team chanted, cheered and circled the three of us like when we were kids playing Little Sally Walker, sitting in a saucer.

"Time to put in work," Coach Todd yells, and we scatter like mice.

Coach has a whole book full of rules, but one in particular is no walking. You have to hustle on and off the field. If Coach Todd catches you walking and you're not hurt, by the end of the next practice, you will be hurting. It will serve as a reminder whenever you feel the need to walk. Traci is the only person that I know who's experienced that punishment twice. She was a slow learner and has aged out of our team.

A few times, I get a glimpse of Coach Ros. She's busy watching us practice and taking notes. We have no clue as to what she thinks about our performance. There are no physical displays one way or another, and we can barely see her face under the visor or behind the sunglasses. We won't learn anything until tomorrow at the next practice.

"YOU'RE LOOKING good out there shortstop," a voice said.

"What in the? You scared me! Jonah, what are you doing here? Are you stalking me?" I rambled off.

"Relax. I am not stalking you. You're feeling yourself, superstar," he said perturbed. "I live in the neighborhood and come here to watch teams practice all the time. I've even watched your team a few times. You're always so focused that you never notice the spectators sitting in the stands or stand along the fence. I did intentionally come today to see if you would be here. I have something for you. Since you wouldn't return my texts or calls, this was the only way I knew to get it to you."

"Give me something like what?"

"A glove conditioner, that's what. I noticed how you keep fidgeting with your glove like you're still trying to break it in. My cousin swears by this stuff and left it at our house. Anyway, I thought you could use it," he said. "But, if you're not interested, I'll take it back."

"Thanks. I had to get a new glove at the start of the season, and I've done everything I know, to break it in, and nothing has worked. I'll give it a try."

"Sure," he said and walked away. Clearly, I struck a nerve, and I feel... I don't know exactly what it is I'm feeling, but there is a sick feeling in my stomach.

"And what are you two old ladies looking at," I rolled my eyes at Jade and Rosie. "I don't want to hear a word from either one of you. Not one word."

"There is no need, other than I told you so." Jade shrugged her shoulders and elbowed Rosie.

"Whatever," I grumbled, walking away from them.

"WHAT ARE you doing over there? That stuff stinks. I'll never be able to fall sleep with that funky smell lingering. You're supposed to do that in a open area, not in a small bedroom with your brother. You're trying to choke me out with the fumes." J.P. fussed.

"Quit whining like a baby. I'm just conditioning my glove. I'm trying to break it in," I said. "Just close your eyes and count sheep, fish, or whatever it is you do to fall asleep. Anyway, I'm almost done and taking the glove outside to cure it all night."

"And you should stay out there with it,"

"No, cry baby."

Grabbing all of my stuff, I head outside to the patio to finish up. Sitting outside in the night air, the crickets and frogs are singing their song. Closing my eyes, I inhale and exhale deeply, appreciating nature's music.

My mind is drawn back to my encounter with Jonah and how he walked away. Though it wasn't intentional, I've identified that feeling I couldn't put a name to earlier. I am disgusted with myself. As much as I hate to admit it, I was a real jackass, and he's due an apology.

I pick up my phone and start a text.

~~Hey. What's up?~~

Nah. That's too personal.

~~*What's up?*~~

Nope. Not it either. Okay, I've got it, keep it simple.

Thanks again for the leather conditioner. This may do the trick this time..

I sat and waited for a response, but there was none. Not even the three dots to show that Jonah's reading the text. So, I sit in silence for ten minutes, hoping he would text back. I decided that if he did respond, I would apologize for being a jackass.

It looks like I will not be apologizing tonight.

I guess it serves me right. After treating Jonah the way I did, I wouldn't talk to me either. Leaving the patio, I locked the back door and made my way through the house.

"Good night," I said to mama and daddy, who were curled up on the couch watching TV.

Passing Gran's room, I stuck my head in the door with intentions of saying good night to her too. She was sound asleep, well she appeared to be. Stiff and very still. I couldn't tell if her breathing was just shallow, or she had stopped breathing altogether. Finally, she took a deep breath and I almost screamed.

Satisfied that Gran was indeed asleep, I tiptoed in and took off her glasses, removed the book from her chest, placing them both on her nightstand, and turned the lamp off. Before I could make it to the door without disturbing Gran, my text notification chimed three times back-to-back and loud enough to wake the dead. Peeping back to make sure it didn't wake Gran.

Stepping into the hall, I opened my phone, fully expecting to see a text from one of my teammates. It's Jonah. Making my way to the, I just sit there afraid to read it.

JONAH: Like I said, my cousin swears by it.

JONAH:SHE also uses it before she puts her glove up for the season.

JONAH:YOU should probably not use it in an enclosed space. It reeks.

ME:GREAT idea. I eventually had to take it outside. It had my room and the hall lit up
    pretty good.

. . .

I GUESS I should apologize for earlier today.

JONAH:OKAY, I'm waiting.

Me:I won't make an excuse, or try to explain, just know that I apologize for being an ass.

Jonah:Apology accepted, I guess. You can make it up to me. I have something in mind.

Me: I'm sure you do.

Jonah: Are you afraid of frogs?

Me: Frogs. Are you serious?

Jonah:Absolutely.

Me:Not exactly. As long as you're not trying to throw them on me, frogs and I are cool.

Jonah:Great. Wednesday night, it's a date. We're going gigging.

Me:Wednesday should be good. Gigging? Are you serious? I've only heard of it but never been. I don't even know anyone that has gone gigging.

Jonah: I am serious. Now you know someone that has been gigging. And don't forget

you're making up for assery behavior, and I get to pick the fun. Make sure you wear clothes you don't mind getting wet and rain boots.

. . .

ME:*I cannot believe I'm agreeing to this. On that note, good night.*

SINCE I HAVE a date with Jonah to go gigging, of all things, it might be a good time to tell my friends. I don't want to hear anything they have to say about Jonah, or any other boy for that matter. We're just going gigging, that's all. Hunting for frogs. Have I lost my mind?

18

———

Today's practice will be different. We are meeting Coach Ros at a gym a few blocks from our practice field. Many of the girls are not exactly excited, but we all want to win.

"Good afternoon, team. Thank you for meeting me here today at the gym. Coach Todd explained that I would be working with you all on strength and conditioning," Coach Ros started. "I've done two evaluations on you all so far, once at your last game, at your last practice. You're an outstanding team, but even good teams can get better. We will achieve this as a team through strength training. I see a hand up. Yes, ma'am."

"Will this strength training give us muscles?" Lydia asked. "I'd like to get ripped."

"That's an excellent question," Coach Ros smiled. "Often, girls question whether these exercises will increase muscle mass because they don't want to get buff. Ocassionally, I get a few who do. These exercises are not to make you buff. They are designed to increase strength and speed."

"We're going to work in four groups of three, and as you noticed, there are four stations set up. Group one, your exercise is goblet squats, group two will perform farmer's walk, group three, you'll be in the far back doing sliding curls, and group four is near the weights for pushup plus. Make your way to your stations, and there is someone there to assist you in getting started. I will float around from group to group. Every ten minutes, we will switch stations."

Rosie, Jade, and I split up in different groups. When it comes to practice, we are serious. We save fun, games, and talking for afterward. Before we knew it, our hour and the workouts were over.

"Good job. Some of you struggled more than others, and that's perfectly okay. It's day one. As you work out more, you will see the difference in what you're able to do and your strength will show up in your game. Practicing at practice alone will only get you good enough. We're shooting for great. See you all tomorrow."

"That workout has me feeling like such a weakling right now," Rosie moaned, as we walked out of the building. "I always thought I was strong, but that workout says differently."

"I might need to take an ice bath, and dunk my whole body," Jade whined. "D.J., you're quiet. Did the workout take your voice?"

"No, the workout did not take my voice," I laughed. "I struggled as much as the two of you."

"Then what's on your mind?" Jade asked. "I know you well enough to know that you're thinking about something."

"Yeah, spill the beans," Rosie backed her up.

"I have a date," I coughed into my elbow.

"Wait. What? Say that again," Rosie stopped walking and grabbed my arm.

"And this time no coughing," Jade said. "You have what?"

"A date. A date. There I said it. I have a date with Jonah," I blurted. "I guess if you can, call it a date."

"I told you he liked you, but you were too busy acting like a weirdo, as if no one could ever like you. When in actuality, all the guys, well, most of the guys like you, and all the girls want to be your friend," Jade fussed.

"And where is he taking you on this *if you call it a date*?" Rosie asked.

"He's taking me gigging," I said, taking a deep breath.

"Gigging?" Rosie questioned. "Ain't that frog hunting?"

"Ewww," Jade said, acting as if something was crawling on her. "Who goes gigging on a date? That is so lame. Can't you get warts from frogs?"

"I think it'll make a great date," Rosie gushed. "One you'll never forget, that's for sure. Come on, Jade. Warts? What grade are you going to?"

"I'm still not one hundred percent sure if it's an actual date," I started to explain. "I was kind of an ass to Jonah and in the spirit of making amends, somehow I agreed to frog hunting. It's very different. So, I'm not sure if it's an actual date or just an outing. Does that make sense?"

"Yes, it makes sense that you are trying to talk yourself out of a date and having a boyfriend," Rosie said. "He's not you know who shall remain nameless, and it's okay that you like someone who obviously likes you back."

We walked in silence a few feet on our way to the practice field. And I let the thought of maybe having a boyfriend dance around in my head. Who are we kidding? Softball is my boyfriend, always has been. Right now, with the absolute most crucial tournament coming up and Gran's dementia, I don't have room for much more.

"Question," Rosie stopped, and with the most serious face asked, "What do you do with the frogs after you catch them?"

In the parking lot of the practice field, we fell to the ground laughing uncontrollably.

"Stooooop!" I scream, trying to catch my breath. "Please, stop laughing. I've gotta pee!"

The three of us have a way of bringing out the best in us and laughing until we can't breathe, and this is one of those times. What would I do without them keeping me grounded, putting me in my place when needed, and being the sisters I never had?

"Come on, ladies. Get the lead out," Coach Todd yelled. "You're not looking like champions today. Surely, you're not going to let one little workout get the best of you."

"No, coach," I yelled. "That work out isn't going to get the best of us. Isn't that right, team?"

My show of confidence in our team was met with

grunts and shrugs. I couldn't get one clear vote of agreement. Coach didn't let up at all. In fact, he dug in deeper. By the end of practice, our tongues we nearly dragging the ground.

"Do I need to tell Coach Ros we don't need her? That we can't handle workouts, and we're not interested in being national champions this year?" Coach Todd yelled.

No one responded. Instead, everyone picked up the pace and practiced through the inevitable soreness. It will be tomorrow's pain serving as a reminder of today's brutal workout.

"Great, because champions are made, not born," coach continued to yell. "Piper, you can't catch the ball with your eyes closed."

The rest of the practice seemed to drag on forever. Dropped balls, missed catches, lazy batting, and no follow-through caused us to repeat drills over and over. It was a never-ending practice. When the coach finally yelled, "Pack it up," there was a unanimous sigh of relief.

"Now I know I'll have to take an ice bath," Jade whimpered.

"Suck it up, crybabies," Rosie yelled, running to the dugout.

19

———

"A re you seriously going on a date?" J.R. asked. "Good for you! See what happens when you're open and not closed off to others?"

"Yeah, yeah," I said, rolling my eyes and not looking back at him standing in the door.

"So, are you going to get dressed?"

"I am dressed," I turned around to give him the full view of my eye and neck roll.

"What do you mean, you are dressed?"

"Just like I said. I am dressed," I repeated.

"From the looks of things, I'd say you're going fishing."

"Close, but no blue ribbon. Jonah is taking me gigging," I tried to sound as if it was a treat. Truth be told, I am terrified that we're hunting for frogs at a pond. If we come across a snake, just bury me right there.

"Gigging? Either this guy is lame, or he's a genius. Please tell me how this goes. I might need to holla at him and learn a little something from him. Gigging," J.R. got a good laugh at my expense.

His laughing was not going to stop me from going. I've never been gigging, and though slightly nervous, I'm interested in the adventure of it all. No one else I know has ever been, other than Jonah, and I think it will be cool. And all of that is bull. I'm just trying to psych myself out.

"There is a very nice-looking young man down-stairs waiting. You'd better hurry up before I take him," Gran said, standing at the bathroom door behind me.

"Thanks, Gran. I'm coming down."

"Don't let your brother's teasing get you down about your date. He doesn't have a date on a weekday or the weekend. Dates should be fun and memorable, not dull and boring. Anyone can go to the movies and dinner, but gigging for frogs, that's a story to tell."

"Thanks, Gran. You always know just what to say," I hugged her.

"I know," she said, laughing and squeezing me just right. "Now, let's get out of here."

We walked downstairs to find Jonah sitting at the kitchen table with my parents J.P. Daddy and mama wanted to know the whereabouts of the pond, and J.P. was far more interested in the frogs.

"D.J., can you bring me back a few frogs," J.P. asked, handing me a jar.

"Absolutely not," mama said, shaking her head and taking the jar from him. "No frogs are coming here, thank you very much."

"How about I take you another time?" Jonah suggested. "You will love it."

J.P. lit up like a Christmas tree. He didn't say a word, just looked at mama for her response. Her eyes were closed as if to say, don't ask her anything.

"On that note, we're leaving," I said, and the two of us headed to the driveway to a beat-up old truck. Jonah opened the passenger door for me and had to slam it a couple of times to make it close.

"I'm glad you didn't chicken out on me," Jonah said as he backed out of the driveway.

"Why would you think I'd chicken out?" I asked.

"The obvious, you being a girl and the fact that we're going to catch slimy and jumpy frogs," he teased.

"There is something you should know about me. I'm always up for a challenge," I explained.

"Is that right? I have a challenge for you. Let's see who can catch the most frogs. There is a legal limit of eighteen."

"Challenge accepted. You're not only going to get beat by a girl, but by a girl who is doing this for the very first time."

"We'll just have to see about that," he laughed.

Laughing and talking during the twenty-minute drive to the pond flew by like the bugs that were hitting the windshield. Pulling off the highway onto a gravel road, Jonah got out to open the gate, drove through, and got out to close it again.

"How do you know about this place? We're not trespassing, are we?" I asked.

"Relax," Jonah smiled, continuing to drive up the gravel road. "This land belongs to my grandparents. They own a pretty large farm; this part of the land is not being farmed. We use the pond for fishing, boat-ing, and gigging. You know, the fun stuff."

"Welcome to Sheffield Pond," Jonah said, pulling up.

"Pond? It looks more like a lake," I said. "Why does it have a name?" I asked.

"Yes, it's definitely a pond. It is named for my

great-great-grandfather for whom legend says dug the pond with his bare hands. My granddaddy says that's just a tall tale that stuck. It was actually here when he bought the land."

"The tall tale does sound better," I laughed.

Jonah let down the tailgate of the truck and reached for the equipment and a cooler.

"Join me," he said, reaching for my hand. "I made us dinner. We can eat and continue to talk while we wait for the sun to go down."

I was completely surprised to find that Jonah did not pack sandwiches. Instead, there were grapes, strawberries, pineapple slices, along with chicken salad, butter crackers, pickles, and bottled tea.

"Do you hear that?" Jonah asked.

"Hear what?" I asked, looking around for what he was hearing.

"Close your eyes and listen," he said with his eyes closed. "The frogs and crickets. It's better than any song or music I've ever heard. When I was little, my grandparents still lived out here on this property. When we went to bed, we'd let up the windows and listen until we fell asleep."

"How's the food?"

"Looks like you put more than a little thought into the meal," I said, nodding in approval. "Let me ask you something. How many girls have you brought here to the Sheffield Pond for gigging?"

"None," he said, looking me square in the eyes and taking a forkful of chicken salad.

"You've never taken any of the Barbie wannabes you've dated gigging before?"

"Unless my little cousin counts. She's the only other girl I've ever taken gigging and she asked a lot fewer questions than you."

"Then why bring me here?" I asked.

"Because you're different from any other girl I've ever met. You're confident, fearless, outgoing, and pretty. I've liked you for a long time, but you've always been so focused on your schoolwork and softball. Finally, I got up enough nerve to approach you, and that article in the paper gave me the in, and a way to get your number.

For a minute, you were knocking down every shot I took. If you hadn't felt guilty about it, I would never have gotten the chance. While I have your attention, I want to show you something that's special to me. I love it here, and it's one of my favorite places to hang out. My grandparents said, one of these days, the farm business and all the land will belong to my cousins and me. I plan to build a house right here on this lake."

"Thank you for the compliment, but you should know that I am very focused on my game right now. I'm not looking to be distracted," I tell Jonah and immediately wished I had just kept my mouth closed. "It's beautiful here. I see why you like it so much,"

"No, distractions," he said real calm and slow. "The sun is going down. Let me show you how to catch with your hands, as well as use a gig."

I nodded in agreement, but in the back of my mind, I knew I had no intention of catching frogs with my hands. The gig will allow me to have more control. At least that's the way it played out in my head. After Jonah showed me both techniques, I'm positive I'll be using the gig.

"Don't forget, this is a challenge. And one I plan on winning," I reminded Jonah.

"Are you ready?" Jonah asked.

"Ready as I'll ever be," I said with a gig in hand and a light strapped to my head.

Jonah leads the way. Right at the edge of the water were cattails and other brush where frogs hid. When my light hit the brush, I was surprised to actually see frogs.

"Only big frogs count," Jonah said. "Those little guys get thrown back."

My first attempt at gigging a frog, I missed and I went down on my knees into the water.

"Are you okay?" Jonah laughed. "While you're down there, grab that frog with your hands."

"I got it! I got it!" I screamed after going for it and grabbing a frog.

"That one's a keeper," he said.

The next two frogs I caught were too little and had to be thrown back. Every frog afterward was huge. I got the hang of it.

"Look at who's a natural," Jonah laughed. "Are you ready to call it a night?"

"Sure. I think I have enough to beat you," I laughed, throwing my net with tonight's catch over my shoulder. We headed back to the truck, where we counted our bounty.

"Winner, winner, frog dinner. My fifteen to your twelve," I danced around. "And who's the winner? Say it. Say it out loud."

"What I didn't tell you is, the winner gets to clean the whole catch," he laughed.

"Jonah Payne, that is not funny. You said nothing about cleaning, only catching. Before I clean them, I'll throw them all back."

"Okay, okay. I'm just kidding," Jonah laughed, and reached for my hand. I didn't jerk away or make any sudden moves. Distraction was setting in, and I wasn't fighting it.

We finished packing up, laughing, and enjoying each other's company.

"Let's get you home before your parents send out a search party," he smiled, opening my door, and slamming it several times. "I hope you had a good time?"

"Surprisingly, I did enjoy myself. Who knew catching frogs would be so much fun?"

"I did," he said. "Thank you for letting me show you a fun time. What would you like to do on our second date?"

20

"D.J. What happened," mama said in a panic when she made it to me in the emergency room.

"While fielding a ground ball during practice, the ball popped out of the glove, hitting her in the face. For a few minutes, she couldn't see. I didn't want to take any chances, so we headed straight to the E.R." Coach Todd explained to mama.

Our wait in the emergency room wasn't long at all. The nurse who wheeled me back said we picked an excellent day to get hurt. No lines and no waiting. I was taken straight to X-ray before going to an exam room or being seen by a doctor.

"Let me see," mama said, taking the ice off my face.

"Oh, Daisy," she said.

"Is it that bad, Mama? You mostly call me Daisy when I'm in trouble, or something is serious."

"Good evening, I'm Dr. Gordon," a deep voice said, introducing himself. "It looks worse than it is. The X-ray shows that the nose is not broken, which is good. But her nose is pretty bruised, as well as shiners on both eyes. Your entire face will probably hurt for a few days."

He shinned his little light in my eyes again, making me look up and down, and from side to side several times.

"There is no sign of a concussion, Daisy. You are lucky the ball missed your mouth. I see a lot of mouth injuries and knocked out teeth due to balls in the face. No practice for a few days, and get plenty of rest," Dr. Gordon suggested.

"No practice? Doc, I have a major tournament to get ready for," I told him.

"I'm not giving you a death sentence. Just a few days of rest to give the swelling time to heal and allow the bruising to start to fade. By the way, your face will be more sore tomorrow, and from the way your coach explained the accident, your neck may be sore as well."

"I can't miss the start of this tournament, Ma. I just can't. Not this time," I pleaded.

"Daisy, that's three weeks away," mama tried to console me. "Let's just focus on healing right now. Okay?"

"Daisy, I don't see any problem with you playing in three weeks. Actually, you can play next week if you're up to it. The bruises might be the only thing you have to show for your unfortunate match with the ball. You might have some pain and discomfort, and I'm prescribing something to help with that. Other than that, you're good to go. And Daisy..."

"Yes," I answered.

"Please be careful and think about wearing a face shield."

"Thanks, Dr. Gordon. We'll take all of that into consideration," mama said. I only nodded because I have no interest in wearing a shield of any kind. I might as well ride the pine.

"THERE IS no way all of you are here?" I said, surprised to find my entire team at the house when I made it there. "Why are you all here?"

"We couldn't go to the hospital, and this was the

only place we could wait for you," Jade said. "There was no way we'd be able to just wait by the phone to hear if you were okay."

"I'm fine," I said in slow motion. The medicine I received in the hospital was starting to make me feel real loopy. "Nothing is broken. My face and ego are both bruised real good, though. Thank you all for caring enough to be here."

"So will you be able to play?" Rosie asked.

"Rosie, don't be so inconsiderate," Zoe hissed.

"I just asked what everyone was thinking. We all want to know," Rosie shrugged.

"Please say yes," Piper said, crossing her fingers.

I nodded and gave a thumbs up. The room exploded with cheers. Understanding their excitement, I smiled from the inside out. We are the definition of all for one and one for all. For this tournament, we need the entire roster.

"Alright, ladies. It's time we head out and let D.J. rest," Coach Todd ordered.

I stood in the doorway with my hand up. Each one of my teammates slapped it as they walked by. Of course, Rosie and Jade were last.

"You know you look like crap," Jade laughed.

"Yeah, I was nervous at first, but you took that

ball to the face like a champ," Rosie teased. "We'll check on you tomorrow."

Finally, I made my way upstairs to rest per the doctor's orders. I don't remember lying down or getting out of my practice gear.

"GOOD MORNING," I heard Gran's voice. "It's time you wake up, eat something, and take your medicine. How's the pain?"

"I have a splitting headache, my neck hurts, my face is throbbing, and I can't make my eyes focus. But I'm here," I smiled. "What time is it?"

"It's just a little past ten," she said. "Your cell phone has been buzzing since about seven this morning. And the house phone has been ringing off the hook since eight. You've even had a delivery this morning, a bouquet of green flowers with a stuffed frog."

"Mmmm," I moaned. It hurt to laugh. "I know who they're from."

"That was sweet. Jonah's a nice young man, and your team is tight-knit. I like that. Now eat as much as you can of this food, and drink this tea with your medicine."

"Yes, ma'am," I agreed, not surprised that she brought me tea. However, I would be surprised if she didn't.

"Is there anything else I can get you?" Gran asked before leaving the room.

"Yes, there is. Can you bring the flowers and frog up? I'd like to see them."

"Coming right up."

"SOMEBODY'S GOT A BOYFRIEND," J.R. said, coming in my bedroom with the flowers and stuffed frog Jonah sent.

"What are you doing? And I don't have a boyfriend."

"I saw Gran about to come upstairs with your gift. I told her I would bring them to you. And yes, if he's sending flowers, he's your boyfriend."

"You have no idea," I said, reaching for the flowers and stuffed frog. The smile that wanted to creep across my face was hard to control. J.R.'s gaze was fixed on me, waiting for my reaction. As nonchalant as I could, I placed them on the night-stand in arms reach, turned my back, and pretended to go back to sleep.

"Gran said to holler if you need anything," he said, exiting the room.

As soon as the door shut behind J.R., I grabbed the frog and the card.

D.J.,

I just want you to know I was thinking about you. I hope this little guy can offer a little comfort while you recover. By the way, I enjoyed our date. You didn't have to get hurt to get out of a second one.

Jonah.

The smile I was repressing made a full appearance. I snuggled up with the frog and replayed our entire date, especially the part where Jonah took my hand.

21

I am super excited because it's my first practice since wrestling with the ball. I was beginning to experience that letdown feeling I get a couple of weeks after the end of the softball season. Although I was at the last two practices and watched, I've missed being out there and getting a good workout. My face feels one hundred percent better, but I still have quite a bit of bruising. I'm not upset about the way I look, but it does bother me that people stare, especially the pesky little kids.

"We're excited to have you back, D.J.," Coach Todd walked over and patted me on the back. "It's not necessary to rush back to it. Your spot is secure." Coach came over to chat before I went out to warm up.

"Thanks for your concern, coach, but I'm good. The doctor has given me the go-ahead, and it's time for me to get back out there."

"If you need to take a little while longer, the team and I will understand."

"Thanks again, I appreciate it," I said, grabbing my glove and trotting to take my spot between second and third base.

Coach Ros was at practice today, and she was batting balls to us. The first few went outfield. My chest started to tighten, followed by coughing. Running back to the dugout, I found my bat bag and pulled my drink out and guzzled it down.

"Are you okay?" Coach Ros asked, stopping me before leaving the dugout.

"I'm fine. It was just a cough. My throat was dry and in need of a drink."

"If you're nervous about getting back out there, just breathe through it."

"Thanks, but I'm fine. Honestly, it was just a dry throat."

I made my way back to my spot between Stormy and Jules, got in the ready position with my feet apart. I staggered, prepared to move, knees bent, body leaning in, and glove ready. Coach Ros hit a ball to me, and I freaked, jumping out of the way of the ball.

"Are you okay? Just breathe." Rosie rushed to me from the pitcher's mound, with everyone's eyes on me.

"Slow down," I heard a voice calling. "Let's talk about it."

"Not today," I responded, snatching up my bat bag and cell phone. Speed dialing my dad, I stood in the parking lot to wait.

"I know what you're going through and I can help," Coach Ros said, walking towards me.

"How could you know? I took a ball to the face, not you."

"No, but I did take a line drive to the gut once at a super-regional during college. I dropped on the pitcher's mound like a fish flopping out of water. I was sore for a while. My coach forced me to return to the pitcher's mound the very next game. He said the best way to get over fear was to conquer it. In the next few games, I walked more than there were actual runs. By game three, coach had no choice but to replace me. I almost lost my scholarship.

It took working with my high school coach that summer, to help me get over my fear of getting hit again. And it didn't take that long. It's more of a lack, or should I say the loss, of confidence, than fear. I know how important the upcoming national tournament is to you. If you allow me, I'd like to help you regain your confidence."

Standing there staring at my cleats, I tried to process all that Coach Ros just said. Line drive, gutshot, loss of confidence, fear, national tournament, regaining confidence. What else do I have to lose?

"I'm in," I mumbled.

"Great, we start tomorrow."

"Tomorrow," I said, finally turning to look Coach Ros in the eyes before opening the door to daddy's car.

"How was practice?" Daddy asked.

I couldn't formulate the words to express how I feel because I didn't know how I felt. My emotions are all over the place. Instead of speaking, I pulled my visor over my face and let my seatback. Holding back the tears made my face burn from the inside out.

"That bad, huh?"

I put my headphones on but didn't turn any music on. It was more of a sign that I didn't want to be bothered than anything. My thoughts were loud enough. Before we could make it home, I had a text from Coach Ros.

Coach Ros: I know I said we'd get started tomorrow, but today is as good as any. I'd like

for you to play catch. While you're playing catch, talk. Talk about anything so that you're not thinking about the ball, just catching.

ME: I can do that.

Coach Ros: That's what I want to hear. If you need to talk, I'm here at any time.

"I'M glad you invited me over, even if is to play catch," Jonah said lobbing the ball to me. "Don't think this counts as a second date. It certainly does not."

"So, tell me more about this lake house you plan on putting on Sheffield Pond one day," I inquired, tossing the ball back to him.

. . .

"DON'T, for one second, think that I don't know what you're up to. Changing the subject doesn't get you out of a second date. I'm always excited to talk about the lake and my plans. We will get back to discussing the second date you promised."

"I PROMISED? I don't remember promising a second date. That was your idea," I laughed. We continued to throw the ball back and forth.

ADMITTEDLY, playing catch didn't initially strike an understanding of how it was going to help me get over my fear of getting hit with the ball. Jonah, just tossing it to me, made me want to throw up. But I refused to show it. As I relaxed, about fifteen minutes in, Coach Ros' exercise started to work. Before I knew it, Jonah had given me a full rundown of his plans for his future lake house, and just as he promised, the conversation made it back around to second date options. All of this while throwing and catching the ball.

"YOU'VE BEEN A GOOD DISTRACTION," I confessed.

. . .

"THERE'S THAT 'D' word again. I'm essential."

"ESSENTIAL? REALLY? YOU'RE FUNNY."

"I ENJOY SPENDING time with you. You're fun, we laugh a lot, and talk about things I've never even considered. I want you to know it will never be my intention to be a distraction to you. In fact, I'll make it my mission not to be."

"THANKS FOR PROVING ME WRONG," I said.

"SAY THAT AGAIN. I didn't hear you clearly. It sounded like you said you were wrong," Jonah moved in closer.

"YOU'RE GETTING TOO CLOSE. You being so close, can't possibly be productive," I tried to step back. The more I stepped backward, the more Jonah stepped forward. It was beginning to look like we were dancing instead of playing catch.

AFTER HE STOPPED MOVING, we continued our back and forth with the ball, Jonah throwing with more heat and speed. I almost didn't realize it because we were enjoying ourselves.

It was about thirty minutes of throwing, catching, and laughing, more laughing than anything, we sat down for a break.

"YOU THIRSTY?" I asked.

"I COULD USE A DRINK. What do you have?"

"WATER, JUICE, AND."

"FRESH LEMONADE," Gran came through the door with a pitcher of lemonade and a couple of glasses. "I've been watching you all for a while and waiting for you to stop so I can bring you something out to drink."

"THANKS, Gran. You didn't have to do that," I said, grabbing the tray from her.

"IT'S MY PLEASURE. I'm just trying to be useful," she winked.

"WHY DON'T YOU JOIN US?" Jonah asked.

"NO, I'll let you two enjoy each other's company," she said, going back into the house.

"HAVE you ever been afraid of something?" I asked, "I mean, like been afraid after something happened?"

"YES. When I was about eight, I almost drowned. My cousins and I were playing around at Sheffield Pond, and my older cousin Calvin double-dog dared me to paddle across the pond on an inner tube. I knew better, and Pop's had told us, time and time again, not to get in the water without an adult around. But Calvin double-dog dared me, so I had to.

I STARTED by behind the inner tube. When I began to get tired, I tried to go under the tube, to get on top of it. That didn't work. Exhausted, I started to sink. Realizing I was about to drown, I panicked. The struggling only worked against me. A hand reached in and scooped me out. I thought it was God. It was Pops, who snatched me out of the water.

I STAYED clear of that pond and any other body of water except a bathtub for a couple of years. Then Calvin double-dog dared me again, this time to swim in the pond. I was so nervous, but I did it, with Pops standing close by, of course. I survived. Little by little, I'd swim a bit more and a little further out."

"I DON'T HAVE three years to get it together. How will I know when I'm ready? Tossing the ball today did not magically cure me of my fear," I confided.

· · ·

"THE BEST I CAN UNDERSTAND, there is no switch or an expiration date on your fear. It will just happen," Jonah tried to reassure me. "Remember how you explained the first time you and Jade made a double play?"

"YES," I nodded.

"DID YOU THINK ABOUT IT?" He asked.

"NO."

"WAS THERE ANYTHING MAGICAL ABOUT IT?"

"NO AGAIN. BUT I CAN'T."

"YOU CAN'T RIGHT NOW. You will when it counts, and you won't even have to think about it," Jonah encouraged.

. . .

"I'M glad you have confidence in me," I said.

"MY CONFIDENCE DOESN'T MATTER. It's the confidence you have in yourself that does."

"HOW DID you get to be so wise?" I asked.

"IT COMES from hanging out with Pops. My granddad has an answer, saying, or a proverb for every situation. I've learned from the best."

"TELL YOUR POPS, thanks. He's brilliant," I laughed.

22

"Outfield," Coach Ros said. "I'm going to hit pop flies to you, catch them and toss them to the side."

My session before practice with Coach Ros was brutal. I thought she was going to take it easy on me. Instead of taking baby steps, she threw me out into the deep end, with no preserver. It was sink or swim. Just walking to outfield, I felt like I was drowning with every step I took.

Jade and Rosie fed her balls, while coach hit them to me over and over again with rapid-fire. I dodged the first three, then turned my back to her to take a breather and get myself together. Coach Ros either didn't get the hint or did not care.

"Turn around and catch the ball," Coach Ros

yelled. "I'm not going to stop hitting them. You either catch or get hit."

With a deep breath and Gran's voice in my head, I heard, *"All the Daisies in our family have been women to reckon with,"* I turned around just in time to jump out of the way of a ball. The next one I caught.

"There you go. Good job," Rosie screamed. "You've got this."

Then I caught another, and another until I got comfortable, and was catching just about all of them. A few balls felt like they were coming too fast.

"Bring it in," coach yelled. "Good job, D.J. I don't mean to take you too fast too soon, but the longer we wait, the more fear settles in and takes over. We have to jump in with both feet, if we want to get ahead of this and have you playing at one hundred percent by nationals."

I nodded, but in my head, I was screaming, NOOOOOO!

"Alright, practice is in ten minutes. Take a breather."

"Coach Ros is a psycho," Jade said, laughing but very serious. "She never stopped hitting balls to you and demanded that we keep tossing them to her."

"You're so dramatic, Jade," Rosie shook her head.

"Actually, she knows what she's doing. I trust her

to help me work through it. If I want to be ready and to do so, and I've got to work for it. I need both of you not to go easy on me. Tough love is what I need right now," I explained.

"You've got this," Rosie said, giving me a high five.

Although it looked like I was talking to my friends, I'm talking to myself and trying to get the three of us on the same page.

The ten-minute break felt more like ten seconds.

"Time to warm up," Coach Todd yelled. "I'm doing something a little different in practice today. Indulge me, please. We're switching it up. All of the infield players are headed outfield, and outfield, you're playing infield. Pick your positions and hustle up, we're wasting daylight."

We all looked around at each other wondering what in the world is going on.

"He cannot be serious," Rosie jogged next to me on our way outfield. "We have a game in two days and we're playing musical positions. I bet Coach Ros has something to do with this. Since she's been on board, we've been doing some weird stuff."

Practice was interesting. I was at center field, Rosie at left field, Jade right field and Jules suited up as back catcher. Being out of place and in someone else's position, gave us a different perspective. Most of all, the switcheroo helped me with my reaction time, giving me an opportunity to think about the ball before it got to me. Unlike being at shortstop, where there is no time to think, just react. Today's practice made me feel like I could play in our upcoming game and contribute.

"Looking good out there, D.J." Coach Ros encouraged. "I hope you all got a feel for your team-mate's positions and came away with a better appreciation, as well as insight of your opponents. Instead of team practice tomorrow, it's individuals before our next game. I will text you the schedule with your time slots. Please be on time. Ladies, one last thing. Keep all distractions to a minimum. We have a lot at stake in the upcoming weeks."

"Distractions, huh? I wonder who she's talking about? Could it be you, D.J.?" Stormy teased, as we walked out of the dugout and headed to the parking lot. "You're all love struck lately. We know that you and Jonah are getting buddy-buddy."

"Distracted and lovestruck, you say? Listen, I'm catching softballs, not feelings," I shot back.

IT'S GAME DAY, and I'm not as nervous as I thought I would be. During my one-on-one with Coach Ros, she said I'd be playing center field this game. What a relief. I hope Piper can handle the pressures of shortstop.

Like every other game, we all arrive at the field listening to music to get our heads in the game. Piper is in the corner of the dugout by herself and looking like she's rehearsing lines to a movie.

"You okay?" I asked.

"I guess so. No, not really, if I'm honest. Secretly, I've always wanted to play shortstop. You get a lot of attention, and I'm usually just hanging out in center field waiting for a ball to come my way. Coach Ros gave me a few pointers yesterday and I'm just trying to remember them. I know which base I'm supposed to back up, but I tend to go in the opposite direction."

"Don't worry. You've got this," I tell Piper. "Trust your instincts, and if you need me, I'm right behind you. I'll be yelling which way to go from center field."

"Bring it in, ladies," Coach Todd yells. "Put in work on three."

"Hey shortstop. Where are you going?" I heard from the other dugout on my way to the outfield. I adjusted my visor and kept jogging to get into posi-tion. Then their dugout starts chanting and laughing.

Hey, D.J.

Hey, D.J.

Tie your shoes

Tie your shoes

Cause Kasey is gonna hit it

Cause Kasey is gonna hit it

Right out to you

Right out to you

Homerun Hitters is one of our biggest rivals and always want to beat us. They haven't won against our team in four years, that's two games per season. So, their eight games behind. News spreads fast in soft-ball. Either they've heard about me getting hit in the face with the ball, and put two and two together, or they're digging at Piper.

"Come on, Diamond Dolls. You've got this," someone yelled from the stands.

The third inning lasted forever. Piper was tired, and after the batter hit the ball directly to her, it was apparent they raddled her cage. She dropped the ball before throwing it to first base. The batter was able to make it safe. That went on player after player after player until the Homerun Hitters had scored three times in that inning alone. They were up six to three.

"Time out," coach yelled and we all met at the mound. "Settle down, Piper. You've got this. You can do it. Tell her D.J. Tell her, she can do it."

"Just take a deep breath, you're doing good," I said, looking her in the eyee. "You're Piper with the plan. You have a plan and don't you forget it."

"Put in work on three," Coach yelled. "One. Two. Three."

"Put in work," we yelled.

Piper went back to position and took the ready stance. The batter hit a ground ball right to her. She scooped it up and tossed it to third base, where there was no runner. She dropped her head, turned around, and headed to center field.

"You're up," Piper said. "You have to play short-stop or we're going to lose to them for the first time in four years."

We bumped gloves I took a deep breath and ran to take my place. Coach Todd was giving me the eye, and Coach Ros came out of the dugout. Both just stared at me.

I nodded at them and remembered what Jonah said, "It's the confidence you have in yourself."

Right now, I'm not very confident, so I'm drawing from the confidence of others.

"Hey, blue, they can't do that," Homerun Hitters' coach yelled.

"Play ball," the umpire yelled back at their coach.

"Welcome back, shortstop," Rosie said.

The other team hit balls deep into leftfield where Lydia was waiting to catch it. The next batter tipped the ball, sending it high in the air over Big Mac's head. Quick, she threw off her helmet, searching the sky for the ball, and catching it for a second out. It was like our momentum and energy changed. Every piece of the puzzle was in its right place.

The next batter stepped to the plate, Burly Bri. She got that nickname a couple of years ago when she hit the ball over the fence. Briana holds an unofficial record in our league for the most home runs. She swung through one time, then pointed the bat into center field, bringing it down to point directly at me. She smiled and her dugout cheered. My heart was pounding so hard. I thought it was trying to beat out of my chest.

Rosie winked at me, then threw Burly Bri two balls.

"Throw me something I can hit," she yelled to Rosie.

I read Rosie's face; I knew it was going to be her curveball before she released it. Bri barely got the bat on the ball, passing Rosie on the mound; the ball was headed between first and second base. Stormy went running for the ball and as I covered second base. She scooped up the ball, lobbing it to Jade on first, but Bri had beat her there and was making her way to second.

Jade threw the ball to me, without hesitating or thinking, I caught it and tagged Burly Bri.

"Oout!" the Umpire yelled.

Jonah was right. It just happened. I ran to the dugout more confident than ever.

"Your breakthrough," Coach Ros said, giving me a high five.

The Diamond Dolls won another game against the Homerun Hitters and sent them on their way until the next softball season.

"Great job, ladies. Next up, nationals," Coach Todd congratulated.

CONNECT WITH ME

THAT'S THE BALL GAME!

On my website: www.larichmedia.com

Facebook: www.facebook.com/larichmedia

Twitter: www.twitter.com/larichmedia

Instagram: www.instagram.com/larichmediagroup

DOUBLE PLAY SUMMER

LATONYA RICHARDSON